Diablo – Race Against Time

Gabi Adam

Diablo –
Race Against Time

Copyright: © 2006 Gabi Adam
Original title: Wettlauf gegen die Zeit
Cover photo: Bob Langrish
Cover layout: Stabenfeldt A/S
Translated by Barclay House Publishing
Typeset by Roberta L. Melzl
Edited by Bobbie Chase
Printed in Germany 2006

ISBN: 1-933343-29-X

Stabenfeldt, Inc.
457 North Main Street
Danbury, CT 06811
www.pony.us

For all those who are involved in the well-being
of animals, without reservations ...

Chapter 1

"Oh, man, school was really awful this morning!" groaned thirteen-year-old Ricki Sulai, as she placed her backpack in the carrier of her bike. "What a break for us the teachers have to get ready to host their district meeting here tomorrow, and gave us this afternoon and all of tomorrow off!"

"You can say that again!" agreed her friend Cathy Sutherland. "Science was unbearable today! I'm so glad we have a few days away from her." The girl rolled her eyes in disgust just thinking about her teacher.

"That's for sure. Is she married, by the way?" Kevin Thomas, Ricki's boyfriend, wanted to know.

"I have no idea, but why do you care?" Cathy looked at him in surprise. "Are you fond of older woman with bad hairdos?"

"Don't be silly! I was just wondering if she's as unpleasant at home as she is here at school."

"Who are you guys talking about?" Lillian Bates, who was slightly older than the others, asked as she joined her friends, completing the close foursome.

"Kevin was just wondering if that grouch we have for a

science teacher has a husband at home we should feel sorry for."

"Ms. Murphy? No, she's an old spinster. And I think she'll always be one!" Lillian laughed as she jumped onto her bike. "Let's get away from this place!"

The four of them pedaled furiously away from the school in order to get home as quickly as possible.

"My house later, at one-thirty?" shouted Ricki to Cathy and Kevin, as they took separate paths.

"Sure!" Kevin called back. "Where else? After all, our horses are in your stable, aren't they?" Kevin grinned, waving to his girlfriend, and then he rode off with Cathy in the other direction.

Ricki and Lillian now pedaled more slowly. The two girls didn't live far apart, just a little beyond the small town where the school was located.

Lillian looked up at the bright blue, cloudless sky. "The weather is fantastic! Let's hope it stays this way for the coming weekend. We don't want the new riding academy's big grand opening event to be rained out.

"The good weather will hold," responded Ricki with conviction, then added, "It's really nice to have a riding academy again, isn't it?"

"It sure is! And about time, too. After all, it's been a while since the old one burned down. But I won't be going there much anymore. It's different when your horse isn't stabled at the riding academy, but boarded someplace else. It's just too much bother. First I have to get to the riding hall, have the riding lesson, and then ride back home."

"Yeah, I feel the same way," agreed Ricki. "And, anyway,

6

nothing beats riding in the countryside on our horses. But every once in a while, a riding lesson is good for us."

"You're right." Lillian wiped her hand across her forehead in the unexpected heat of the Indian Summer day. "I didn't register Holli for a single event this year! I'm totally out of practice, but just the same, I'd like to participate in some way."

Ricki looked at her girlfriend questioningly. "But what could we do if we don't take part in the jumping or the equestrian events?"

"Oh, I don't know! Maybe I just want to enjoy the excitement of the exhibitions."

"Well, then it should be enough just to go as spectators, shouldn't it?"

"Yes … No! That doesn't seem right, somehow," answered Lillian and shrugged her shoulders. "Oh, just forget it! I think my brain isn't working today," she joked, grinning.

Ricki laughed. "Maybe an afternoon ride through the countryside will clear your brain."

"Let's hope so! Anyway, see you later."

"Yeah. I can't wait! 'Bye!"

The anticipation of going riding put Ricki in such a good mood that she almost flew the last few yards home on her bike. She leaned her bike against the side of the garage, grabbed her backpack from the bike carrier, and ran straight to the stable.

"Do you have a rocket tied to your backside, young lady? Or are you just afraid that Diablo will get cranky if you bring your school bag into the house first?" teased Jake, the elderly stable hand. He got out of the way just in time, as Ricki came bolting through the door.

"Hello, Jake! 'Scuse me, I'm just so glad to be away from that boring school for a few days! How's my sweetie?" Ricki threw her bag into the corner of the stable and ran over to her horse's stall.

Diablo greeted her with a low, soft whinny.

"My boy, I've missed you soooo much! How are you?" Ricki gave him a big kiss on his velvety muzzle and then searched her pockets for a treat for him. "Sorry, Diablo. I'll have to give you something later. I completely forgot that I still have my school clothes on." She patted his muscular neck comfortingly, and stroked the long black mane hairs back from his eyes.

Lillian's Doc Holliday whinnied jealously. *Hey, what about me? I'm here, too, you know*, he seemed to be saying, and Ricki went from one stall to the next, laughing, greeting all of Diablo's stable mates.

Sharazan, Kevin's beautiful roan, had as much of a sweet tooth as Diablo, and he turned away from Ricki, disappointed that she hadn't brought him anything either, as she usually did.

Rashid, Cathy's foster horse, snorted contentedly into the girl's hair. The dun was a very gentle animal. He belonged to the former circus rider Carlotta Mancini, and, together with Sharazan, came from a small circus that had to be closed down due to financial difficulties.

"Hey, you two. Everything okay?" Ricki was now standing in front of the last stall, from which two pairs of mischievous eyes looked out at her. Chico, the little donkey who belonged to Lillian's family, and Salina, a pony mare, who also belonged to Carlotta, were standing side by side. Ricki thought they always looked like they were planning some prank.

"You guys are the best!" she praised the two animals, while she rubbed their heads behind the ears.

Diablo whinnied loudly.

"Don't worry, Diablo. You don't have any competition!" the girl laughed, before she sighed and picked up her school bag and looked down at her clothes. Greeting the horses had left obvious traces on her new T-shirt and newly washed jeans.

"Mom will be so ticked off," she mumbled to herself, as she tried to get rid of the worst spots with her handkerchief. Of course, that didn't work.

Oh, well! That's what washing machines are for, she thought, as she rushed past Jake and ran into the house, where her mother, Brigitte, had already put lunch on the table.

"Hey, Mom!" called Ricki as she hurried into the bathroom to try to remove the dirt from her school clothes with water – and avoid a storm of criticism from her mother.

"Hello, Ricki! Were you in the stable again with your clean clothes? I've told you over and over that you should – At least wash your hands before you sit down to eat!"

Oops! the girl thought, returning to the bathroom. Then she appeared in the kitchen with an apologetic smile on her face. She looked around, searching. "Is Dad here?"

"No. He drove to Grandma's with Harry about fifteen minutes ago!"

"What? I wanted to go to Grandma's too! It's always Harry who gets to go! That's so unfair!" pouted Ricki, and she plunked herself down onto a chair at the table. She picked at her tuna salad disinterestedly.

"We thought you'd probably want to go riding today."

"Well, that's true, but –"

Brigitte leaned against the sink, an exasperated look on her face. "You always say that you want to go, but an hour after you get there you're always itching to get back home. So why are you complaining?"

Ricki looked a little insulted. "I'm not!"

"Then everything's okay! I'm sure your friends will arrive shortly and you'll all disappear for the rest of the day somewhere in the area or at the very least in the stable!"

Her daughter laughed at that. "You're right! We're probably going to ride over to Carlotta's today. We want to see how far the workers have gotten with the renovation of the horse ranch. She wants to open her doors to old horses before the end of the year."

"Say hello to her for me, and if she has time and wants to, ask her to come by some day this week for coffee and cake." Brigitte dried her hands on a dishtowel and left the kitchen.

"Okay, Mom!" called Ricki after her, and then she quickly ate her lunch. The thought that she would soon be riding to the ranch with her friends put her in a great mood.

*

"I was beginning to think you guys weren't coming," said Ricki, as the teens saddled up.

"Well, we can't fly," Cathy responded sharply.

As the girls mounted their horses, Lillian asked, "Are we going to ride to Carlotta's, or do you have another suggestion?"

10

"Carlotta has enough to deal with, overseeing the construction workers. I think we'd just be in the way," replied Kevin, cinching the girth around Sharazan. "What about riding over to the Hartmans again?"

Ricki laughed out loud. "You're such a chow hound! You're just drooling over that fabulous frosted lemon pound cake that Mrs. Hartman makes, aren't you?"

"You bet I am! Today is Thursday, and if I remember correctly, she always bakes on Thursdays," admitted the youth, as his eyes took on a dreamy look. "Just thinking about that freshly baked lemon pound cake makes my mouth water! Especially with strawberry jam ... mmm, delicious! I can't get it out of my head!"

"Well, if that's the way it is, then we'd like to help you out a little!" responded Ricki, and winked at her friends.

"Yeah!" agreed Lillian.

"Let's go!" shouted Cathy, while Kevin looked from one to the other, completely bewildered.

"What are you guys planning?" he asked as the girls shrieked and urged their horses into a gallop. "Hey, are you crazy? Hey!" Sharazan bounded forward while Kevin tried to get his foot into the stirrup, which had slipped out from under him.

"Just wait! I'll get you for that!" he called after the girls, who disappeared behind the trees, laughing.

Kevin stopped his horse and thought it over. If he took a shortcut, he could make it to the Hartmans' farm before they did. He guided Sharazan quickly to another path and let him gallop. He'd show those girls!

He and his horse raced along for a few minutes, while he forgot everything else around him. But suddenly he came upon several tree stumps lying across the path, and Sharazan stopped short, bringing him back to reality.

"Darn," he mumbled to himself, disappointed. It was clear that he wasn't going to beat the girls this way. He turned his horse around, annoyed, and rode back to the starting place at an easy trot.

It didn't take long for the girls to return as well.

"Hey, did something happen? How come you didn't follow us?" shouted Ricki from a distance. Kevin just shrugged.

"The other path was blocked. It just goes to show you shouldn't ever try to take a shortcut on horseback!"

"Oh, you were going to cheat, were you? Well, then, you'll get a cheater's reward," grinned Ricki. "The Hartmans aren't home! That means you can forget about that cake!"

"See! I knew that, which is why I didn't ride after you," claimed Kevin, but nobody believed him.

"You liar! That'll cost you a soda! At least! You can't lie to your girlfriend without consequences!" responded Ricki.

Lillian added immediately, "And you can't lie to the girlfriends of your girlfriend either! We get sodas, too!"

Kevin groaned. "Hey, girls, lighten up, have a heart. How can you take advantage of a poor guy who doesn't have much money?"

"Don't complain. It's your own fault!"

"We could go to Nico's later this afternoon for pizza. What do you think?" suggested Cathy.

"Great idea!" the others agreed.

"Want to ride over to the new riding hall?" asked Lillian.

"What do you want to do that for? You don't want to ride around in the sandpit on such a nice day, do you? We'd probably get our lungs filled with dust!" Cathy shook her finger in protest.

"I don't want to take a riding class. I just want to have a look around."

"Then okay, if all you want to do is look."

The four riders turned and rode off in the direction of the newly constructed riding academy, which would be officially opened that weekend, at the riding exhibition.

*

"Hey, guys, look! That's Crissy and Maggie over there! We haven't seen them in ages! Hello!" Ricki stretched upward a little in Diablo's saddle and waved frantically to the other two riders, who were exercising their horses in the newly landscaped area around the riding hall.

"Ricki! Hey! It's great that you guys have finally taken the time to drop by." Crissy rode over to the gang on her horse, Evening Star, while Maggie just nodded at them and kept her horse Giaccomo going toward the medium-high jump that was set up in the middle of the ring.

The others watched closely as the big chestnut horse sprang over the obstacle with a huge jump and landed safely on the other side.

"Is Maggie practicing for the show?" asked Lillian, and Crissy nodded, a look of anxiety clouding her face.

"Is something wrong? Why do you look so weird all of a sudden?" Ricki asked with concern.

"Maggie has a problem," Crissy whispered softly. "But she would kill me if I told you about it."

Ricki turned to Crissy, "Just tell us, we won't tell anyone!"

"Well … okay." The girl looked back over her shoulder to make sure that Maggie was out of earshot. "She's under a lot of pressure. Her father has threatened to sell Giaccomo if she doesn't win at least second place in the jumping event. He said, in so many words, 'That beast is worthless and just costs us money.' And he recently made a big fuss when Maggie got careless and took a fall off Giaccomo. He said that Giaccomo threw her off on purpose. In other words, the horse is also dangerous. Her dad swore that he would have the animal put down if she fell off one more time!"

Even Kevin-the-jokester turned serious at that threat. "Is he crazy? That's illegal. No vet in his right mind would agree to put down a healthy horse. And besides, do you know any riders who've never fallen off their mounts? And Giaccomo is really dependable! If anyone falls off him, it's their own fault!" he exclaimed angrily.

"Tell me about it! We know that, and just about everybody knows that, but Maggie's father doesn't give a hoot! If he decides to do something, there's no stopping him. I can't bear thinking about what will happen if Maggie falls off her horse in the jumping event on Sunday! But she has no choice. She has to participate in the advanced level competition in order to prove to her father that Giaccomo is a great show horse."

"But Maggie isn't very good at jumping, if I remember correctly," Cathy said softly. "She'll never make it through the advanced course with no mistakes! Remember how tough it was for her to make it through the riding exam? A beginning jump is okay for her, maybe even an intermediate, but an advanced with no mistakes? I don't know. I think

Giaccomo could do it, but Maggie? And when was the last time she even went through an official jumping course?"

"That was a long time ago. And she only took the test to show her Dad that he could be proud of her. But it didn't work. And you don't know this, but she's always been scared of jumping, she just doesn't admit it! That's the second problem! She's probably going to lose Giaccomo no matter what she does. She doesn't have the nerve to survive an advanced course. And the chances that she'll stay in the saddle for all the jumps are one in a million!"

"That's really awful! Isn't there anything that can be done? Is her father really so stubborn?"

Crissy shrugged her shoulders sadly as she watched Maggie repeatedly guide Giaccomo to the steep jump.

"You know what? I think he's jealous of the horse. He was always the most important person in Maggie's life. But ever since she got Giaccomo, she spends more time in the stable than she does at home. That puts Mr. Bratton a little farther down on the list of idols in her life. And he doesn't seem to be able to get used to that," explained Crissy.

"Jealous?" asked Lillian, shaking her head in amazement. "Of a horse? That man must have a screw loose! If my dad was jealous of Holli, I think my mother would have him committed to a loony bin!"

"And I would just ride off with Diablo if my father threatened to sell him or – worse – have him put down," added Ricki with a defiant expression on her face.

"As though it were that easy," replied Kevin with a dismissive gesture.

"Shhh! She's coming!" whispered Crissy and put a smile

on her face. "Hey, the jumps were really great! If you do as well on Sunday, you'll probably win a trophy!"

Maggie tried to smile. "It would be wonderful, but I don't think it's going to happen. Hello, by the way. It's great to see you guys again! Your horses look fabulous!"

"Giaccomo isn't bad either! He's as shiny as a new penny." Ricki beamed at the rider on her brown horse, but her heart sank. The idea that this wonderful horse could fall victim to a lethal injection was unbearable to her. What a horrid man this Mr. Bratton must be if he could threaten a thing like that.

"I have to win, otherwise … otherwise he's going to be sold," said Maggie quietly. Her eyes filled with tears. "I ... I won't be able to stand it if he's taken away!" Jerkily she turned her horse on his hind legs and bolted away across the sandy ring. She didn't want them to see her crying.

Ricki frowned. "What do you guys think? There must be a way to prevent that! We can't just stand by and let Maggie lose her Giaccomo."

"But what can we do beyond hoping and praying and keeping our fingers crossed that she wins the jumping event?" answered Crissy dejectedly.

"Well, that really isn't much. No, we have to come up with something, maybe something that also proves to Mr. Bratton that Giaccomo isn't dangerous," suggested Ricki.

"Yeah, and then? He still won't think he's worth anything, and that's so unfair. It's not Giacco's fault that jumping isn't Maggie's strong point!" Lillian shook her head again.

"Hey, Crissy, we're getting together later this afternoon at Nico's for pizza," volunteered Ricki. "Can you get Maggie to come with you? Maybe, if we all put our heads together, we'll be able to think of something to help her."

"Good idea." Crissy looked at Ricki gratefully. "I'll try to get Maggie to come, but I can't promise anything. I have a feeling that she wants to enjoy every free moment with Giaccomo while she still can."

Cathy was close to tears herself. She was hit by Maggie's misery, too.

"Well, see you later!" Ricki took one last look at Maggie, who had her head down and was riding around and around the ring with her horse. It was as though the girl had already given up hope that she would be able to keep her horse. She knew she didn't stand a chance of going against her father's wishes.

*

Dejectedly, the four friends left the area surrounding the riding academy. Giaccomo's uncertain future made all of them sad.

"What happened to you?" Jake asked when he met up with the kids in the stable as they were silently unsaddling their horses.

"Mr. Bratton happened," answered Kevin brusquely.

"I don't understand, but maybe that has something to do with my age," commented Jake, after no further explanations were forthcoming. Shrugging his shoulders, he started sweeping up the corridor in the stable, and he glanced at the four teenagers with squinted eyes, as they jumped on their bikes and disappeared down the road toward town.

I hope they're not in some kind of trouble again, the old man thought, and turned to his favorite, Diablo. "Can you tell me what's going on with them? No? Of course, not! I didn't expect you to." Lovingly, he stroked the black horse across the small white blaze on his forehead, which was hidden under the long mane.

*

As the friends approached the pizza parlor, they were beginning to feel a little better. They were convinced they would find a way to help Maggie keep her Giaccomo. At the moment, they had no idea how they were going to do that, but just the thought of helping was enough to cheer them up.

"Hey, we look really grubby! Can we go in there looking like this?" Ricki looked down at her clothes doubtfully.

"Nico is used to it. We always look like this when we've been riding," responded Lillian. "No one pays any attention anymore."

"Okay, if you say so, then let's get going. I'm hungry!"

The wonderful smells of Italian cooking wafted toward them as they opened the door.

"Heavenly! People should have at least three stomachs. One for pizza, one for spaghetti, and one for lasagna," announced Kevin, grinning.

"And one for Alka-Seltzer afterward, if you begin to feel miserable," added Cathy.

The kids plopped down at their favorite round table in the corner, right beside the counter.

Nico leaned over the counter. "Madonna mia!" he said, a

big smile on his face, "you kids look like tramps! If you have so much hunger, I can close my pizzeria. I'll be sold out! What'll it be? Your usual?"

"The usual!" the answer came back immediately.

"With lots of pepperoni and mushrooms," Kevin added.

"*Certo!* Francesca, the European, large, with extra pepperoni and mushrooms and four colas."

"Aha! The young riders are here. Is Kevin's stomach grumbling again?" Nico's wife, the plump Francesca, stuck her head through the sliding window to the kitchen and waved to them warmly.

"Hey, Francy!" Ricki waved back and grinned at Nico, who once again held his hands on his head in exasperation. "Francesca is such a beautiful Italian name and you say always Francy! You Americans have no ear for the Italian language, which is the language of music! You have no patience ... always using abbreviations."

"Oh, Nico, don't take it so seriously! If you were as hungry as we are, you'd abbreviate, too!" responded Cathy, and then she pointed out the window. "Look, guys, Crissy and Maggie are coming."

"I'm so glad that Crissy managed to get her to come along," Ricki said, genuinely happy as the two girls joined them at their table.

"Hey! You got here just in time. We just ordered."

"Great," said Crissy and pulled two more chairs over to the table.

"I'm not really hungry," Maggie said softly.

"Don't be ridiculous! With all these delicious smells in here, it's impossible not to be hungry," answered Kevin, in a tone that didn't allow any objections.

19

Maggie gave up and the two new arrivals ordered pizza as well.

*

About forty-five minutes later, after the kids had finished their pizzas, Kevin leaned back, satisfied, and announced, "All I need now is more food. I feel like I could burst!"

"If you're still hungry, Kev, I'll pay for the spaghetti," said Ricki, winking at the others.

"Thanks, I'm completely full. Cheers!" The teenagers toasted each other by clinking their soda glasses together.

After taking a sip from her soda, Maggie asked softly, "Are you all going to participate at the show?"

Kevin almost choked. "No! Absolutely not! The most Cathy and I could manage would be a circus dressage."

"And I'm completely out of practice, not to mention Holli," responded Lillian.

Ricki sensed that Maggie was looking at her and shook her head. "No thanks! Remember two years ago, when I was allowed to ride Chantal for the first and last time, and she suddenly turned ninety degrees in front of the spread-fence jump? Good grief, I'll never forget it. I went flying right off the horse in full gallop and landed outside of the course, involuntarily."

Cathy giggled. "Disqualified due to leaving the course. That was great! No one besides you managed such a skillful performance that day. Chantal raced to the start, dumped you in slow motion, and then raced around the course over and over, jumping the hurdles with no effort every lap. I think, after a quarter of an hour –"

Ricki groaned. "Okay, already! Don't remind me of all the grim details. Oh, that was so embarrassing! I think I'm just not made for shows. But I love the atmosphere and, like Lillian, I'd like to – Wait a minute!" Ricki stared at the neighboring table, where a young man was sitting with a small boy, trying to show him how to eat spaghetti. Unfortunately, the youngster didn't seem to be hungry.

"Hey, I have an idea! And you can all do it with me," said Ricki,

"Huh? What are you talking about? At the show? We just said that we'd –" began Kevin.

"Show yes, but no dressage or jumping," Ricki interrupted her boyfriend and grinned at Lillian, as she remembered their earlier conversation. "I have an idea!"

"I think you must've been bitten by some big black horse. You're talking in riddles! What else can you do at a show? Sell hot dogs or cold drinks? Are you interested in working all of a sudden, instead of riding?" Cathy looked a little skeptical.

"Oh, don't be ridiculous! Someone else can sell lemonade and hot dogs. That's not my thing," replied Ricki. "I was thinking of something completely different. We could organize a riding ring for children, but –"

"Riding for children?" Kevin rolled his eyes. "Can't you come up with anything better than that? Do you really want to run around in the sun with whining little kids? Your ideas are getting weirder and weirder. Hey, Nico!" he called to the owner across the room. "What did you put into the pizza? Ricki is acting weird!"

Nico hurried over to their table. "Ricki, are you feeling

sick? Francesca is making the pizza just like always! I calling doctors, you not paying for dinner! Francy, call the emergency!"

Kevin and the girls burst out laughing. They were doubled over from giggling and pounded the table with their hands so that it began to wobble dangerously.

Nico looked from one to the other, confused. "Francesca, don't call the emergency, call the doctors at the loony bin. Guests here in our restaurant are going crazy!"

Kevin laughed until he cried. "Nico" he panted. "Nico, you ... you called her Francy! I think you're losing your sense of the beauty and music in the Italian language in small-town Pennsylvania!"

Nico wanted to say something, but decided against it. He threw a dishcloth in mock fury at Kevin's head. Everyone in the restaurant was laughing. People always had fun at Nico's.

After the silly episode had ended, Lillian still wanted to know what Ricki was planning.

"Well, listen up. This is my idea. We organize a riding ring for children at the show on Saturday and plan to spend the entire day. We could take turns saddling our own horses, two hours at a time, and let the children ride them. For one time around, we could charge, well, let's say, hmm, a dollar!"

"And we can pay for our dinner out of that! Genius idea!" Kevin was enthusiastic.

"Idiot! All you ever think about is eating! The money that we earn will be donated to the orphanage. I thought we could paint a big sign – Kids Ride for Kids. The parents would be too embarrassed not to participate!"

Kevin and the others were speechless.

22

"Since when have you become such a do-gooder? Do you often have ideas like this?" he asked, amazed, and Ricki nodded strongly.

"Of course! We'll kill two birds with one stone! First, the orphanage will be happy, and second," – she looked directly into Maggie's eyes – "second, we can prove to Maggie's father that Giaccomo is one of the gentlest horses in the world, provided that Maggie lets some kids ride her brown horse!"

The girl turned pale. "That ... that's really ... you are really ... a genius!" she stammered, happy and relieved. "Dad will never be able to say that Giaccomo is dangerous again, and then there would be no reason to sell him, unless –"

Crissy put her hand on her friend's shoulder and gave her a little shake. "Don't say anything!" she begged her.

Maggie looked down and nodded almost invisibly, while the others toasted each other again and clinked glasses.

"To Ricki!" said Kevin proudly. "That's the best idea you've had in hours!"

"To our project, Kids Ride for Kids, whatever comes of it," Lillian offered a second toast.

Ricki repeated, dramatically, "To the project, and to Maggie keeping her Giaccomo!"

Chapter 2

The following day, Maggie sat in her parents' kitchen lost in thought, oiling the same spot on her saddle over and over again with an old rag. She was thinking about Giaccomo, especially the threats her father had made, but also about the latest fight with her father about cleaning up her room.

"Maggie, are you daydreaming?"

Jolted from her thoughts, the girl jumped nervously. "What did you say, Mom?"

"I said you'd better hurry up, or your father will be furious when he gets home!" Mrs. Bratton was going to add something, but just then the phone rang.

"Let me get it! It's probably for me!" Maggie stumbled over the separate parts of her snaffle and reached for the receiver.

"Bratton resid – oh, darn!" The girl had tried to lean against the counter and lost her balance. She bumped into the coffee maker, knocking it to the floor.

At the other end of the line, there was loud laughter. "Greetings, Miss Bratton. This is Crissy. What's up?"

"I was just spreading coffee grounds all over my freshly oiled snaffle. It looks great, all spotty! Now I'll have to start all over again!"

"Hey, I talked with Vince. The children's riding ring is all set! He got in touch with the board of trustees, and they thought it was a terrific idea. But we knew that anyway! The project only enhances the image of the riding club. I can just imagine the newspaper article they'll write. 'Avalon Riding Academy has begun a project to support the local orphanage!' By the way, Vince wanted to know if you're planning to come to jumping class tonight, to prepare for Sunday with Giaccomo."

Maggie closed her eyes. She was more than grateful to her riding instructor for his offer, but she knew that the jumping lesson would just make her more anxious about the competition. The pressure on her would certainly cause her to make mistakes, and every obstacle she knocked over would undermine her self-confidence.

"In case you see Vince before I do, please tell him I said thanks, but that I don't think it would do any good," she answered softly.

"Well okay, if that's what you think. When will you be finished there? We promised Ricki we would make that poster and stuff."

"Oh, my gosh, I completely forgot about it! Wait a minute ... probably the best thing would be for me to come to your house right now. I can oil this thing tonight. See you soon."

"Okay, see you."

Maggie hung up the receiver and turned to her mother, who knew exactly what was coming.

"Oh, no! You can't just leave all this stuff lying here. You promised to clean up before your father gets home."

"But, Mom, we have so much to do for tomorrow. You know how it is. Couldn't you –?"

"No, I couldn't! Look at this mess! Coffee grounds all over the place ... cloths, rags, leather polish, sponges, leather straps, saddle –"

"But, Mom, it's for a good cause. Think of the children we want to help, and think of ... think of Giaccomo! Mommy, please!"

Mrs. Bratton sighed loudly. Maggie had found her weakness. If it was for a good cause, she just couldn't say no, and as far as Giaccomo was concerned ... well, she really liked her daughter's horse.

"All right, go! But you have to help me in the garden next week, is that clear?"

"I promise! You're the best! See you later." Maggie gave her mother a big kiss on her forehead and then took off before her mother could change her mind.

Mrs. Bratton shook her head and smiled. Then she looked at the mess and decided to have a cup of coffee before she began cleaning it all up.

*

"We need to paint a sign that attracts everyone's attention. Let's put it at the entrance where Tyler and Anne will be sitting to collect the money." Maggie sat cross-legged on Crissy's bed and watched her search her room for a sketchpad.

"Now where did I put that thing? I'm positive I saw it up

there on the shelf a few days ago. Now it's gone! Let's see if Jeff has one in his room." She ran quickly over to her little brother's room and came right back.

"I thought so. Of course he has one. Mine! Little brothers are a disaster!"

Maggie looked at her pensively. "I wouldn't know about that. I wish I had brothers and sisters. I wouldn't even care if they were older or younger. It's not that great being an only child."

"Yeah, yeah, the spoiled only child," teased Crissy, and got a pillow thrown at her head.

Right away a boisterous pillow fight ensued, which ended only when Crissy's mother entered the room.

"Is this the way young women act when they want to be treated like grown-ups? It sounds like the ceiling's about to fall down!" Mrs. Marshall looked accusingly at the two girls.

"Who's grown up?" asked Crissy innocently, and Maggie added, "Where do you see women here?"

"Oh, you kids!" Mrs. Marshall laughed.

"It's okay, Mom, we'll stop!" promised Crissy and sat down on her blue slipcovered bedroom chair like a proper young woman.

"Dear Miss Margaret," she sang prissily. "Would you be so kind as to join me?"

"Of course, my dear," Maggie played along, bringing over the desk chair. "By the way, your pillows are flying very well today. My compliments!"

Both girls broke out in laughter, and Crissy ended up in a fit of coughing.

"Maggie, I can't stand it! Stop it!"

"I can't."

For a while, both of them kept bursting out laughing, until, finally exhausted, they calmed down.

"We'd better get started with the sign."

"You're quite right, my dear!" And that started them up again. It took them a while before they could get down to business and think clearly.

"Maybe we could just paint a large red ball and write around it, 'Kids Ride for Kids.' After all, the board decided the money's going to the Red Ball Orphanage," suggested Crissy, but Maggie shook her head.

"That's much too simple. Hmm, wait a minute, I have an idea." She grabbed the sketchpad and made a rough drawing.

"Hey, wow, that looks great!" Crissy said enthusiastically. "Keep going."

After a while Maggie said, "I think it could look something like this! Now we're getting somewhere. Did you get the large piece of white poster board and the paint?"

"Yeah, but if it rains, the whole painting will be ruined."

"If it rains, we won't do the kids' riding anyway, and then the whole thing with Giaccomo will be ruined, too! Give it to me! It just *has* to be good weather!"

"That's true! Come over here to my desk. That's where I keep everything."

While Maggie drew for about two hours, Crissy polished her tack.

"You're so lucky. I still have to do that tonight! Man, I hope Mom was able to clean up my mess before Dad got home. Otherwise, I can look forward to a huge scene tonight."

"I'll come with you and be your backup, okay? And I'll also help you with polishing your gear. I'm already in practice." As proof, Crissy held up her two greasy hands.

"Terrific," responded Maggie. "Will you come help in the garden next week, too?"

"How come?"

"Because I had to promise my mother that I would weed the garden one day next week if she would clean up my mess."

"Okay, I'll come help you in the garden, too! Your mother's really cool, by the way," exclaimed Crissy enviously, and then both girls grew silent again. Maggie had to concentrate so that she didn't make any mistakes.

About ten o'clock at night, Crissy's father dropped off the two girls at the Brattons' apartment. Maggie opened the door quietly and slipped into the relatively dark hallway with her girlfriend.

"What's going on here?" The girl heard someone snoring and looked at Crissy, confused. Cautiously she peered into the living room and discovered her father, who was mumbling something in his sleep.

"Oh no, there must have been a fight because of the mess in the kitchen! Come on, Crissy, let's get out of here."

They tiptoed into Maggie's room. The saddle and the snaffle lay on the floor, separated into shiny parts. Next to them there was a note:

You'll have to put this all back together yourself. I have no idea where everything goes. I hope everything goes really well with your project. Good night, Mom

"Now I know what happened," sighed Maggie. Dad caught her polishing my saddle for me and freaked out.

29

Uh-oh, that means trouble. I just hope he doesn't sell Giaccomo right away."

Crissy took a deep breath. "Don't think of the worst-case scenario! Tomorrow is a new day, and your dad will have calmed down by then for sure! You know what, let's buckle up your saddle and the snaffle, and then let's go to bed. If it's okay, I'll stay over tonight, and stick up for you tomorrow, in case of trouble. Just let me call my parents."

"You're a real pal, Crissy. Thanks!" Maggie embraced Crissy and gave her a hug, and then they got started with the leather straps, which were all tangled up. After a while, the two of them fell into bed, dog tired, and hoped that they would hear the alarm the next morning.

*

In Ricki's room, two sleeping bags were on the floor, and Lillian and Cathy were trying to get comfortable on them. In order to get into her bed, Ricki had to climb over her friends.

"I told you it would be a little crowded," she said apologetically.

"Oh, we're fine!" grinned Lillian. "If I don't think about my back, which will probably be stiff tomorrow, I feel just great!"

"You can sleep in my bed, and I'll sleep on the floor," offered Ricki, but Lillian just waved her away.

"Too bad we're not allowed to sleep in the stable," commented Cathy, a little sadly. She had imagined herself bedded down on soft hay. The friends had decided to spend the night at Ricki's so that they could all get an early start for the show grounds together.

30

"You know what Jake said? That we would probably talk half the night and disturb the horses. He said if we slept in Ricki's room, then at least the animals will have gotten their rest and be fit in the morning!"

"Us? Talk half the night? What would make Jake think that?" laughed Cathy, grinning.

"Exactly. I asked myself the same thing. By the way, how late is it, anyway?" asked Lillian.

"Two-fifteen!"

"Did we spend all that time in front of the computer?"

"Stop it! If my mother knew, it would be the last time you'd get to spend the night here," whispered Ricki before she finally turned out the light.

"Do you think that Maggie will be able to keep Giaccomo?" asked Lillian quietly, her eyes already half closed.

"Let's hope so," whispered Ricki in reply, before she fell into a deep, dreamless sleep.

*

"Oh no, it can't be time to get up!" Crissy groaned and felt around for the beeping alarm clock on the stand next to the bed. Maggie jerked awake suddenly as the light went on.

"What? Is it time to get up already? Oh, man, that was a short night. I'm dead tired." She yawned and stretched and then closed her eyes again.

"Hey, you sleepyhead. Get out of bed." Crissy shook her girlfriend by the shoulder. "We have to get up! Did you forget? Today is Saturday."

"Saturdays are for sleeping late. There's no school!"

"Wow, you really are still half asleep. Today's the horse show! The horse show!"

Quick as lightning, Maggie sat up and bumped her head on the shelf above her bed.

"Ouch!"

"Well, at least now you're awake." Crissy grinned as Maggie rubbed her sore forehead.

"Darn it, now I'll get a bump!"

"Press a quarter on it, that helps."

"A quarter? I wish I had one!"

"Oh, you poor little only child!" Crissy teased her girlfriend.

"Stop saying 'child.' That makes me think of my father!"

"Oh, gosh, I'd forgotten all about him. I'm sorry."

"Who? My father?" Slowly, the pain eased and Maggie began to gather up her riding gear.

"No, my thing about only children!" Crissy was almost finished dressing, while Maggie was still scrutinizing her riding pants.

"Well, these should have been washed."

"Why don't you just brush them off with a damp brush? By the time we get organized, they'll be dry," suggested Crissy. "It's just for the kids' riding ring. Your white show pants are clean, aren't they?"

"Of course, what do you think?" Maggie disappeared into the bathroom with her riding pants and came back after a few minutes with wet spots all over them.

"I can't wait to see how they look when they're dry. If I have to, I'll just say it's the latest trend! Ugh!" Maggie made a face. "Do you want to have breakfast?"

"It wouldn't hurt. At least I wouldn't mind some juice and toast."

"Okay, then come with me. Let's see if my father's still sleeping in the living room."

"Hey, what about having breakfast at my house?" offered Crissy. "I mean, then you wouldn't have to worry about your father," she said, but Maggie just shook her head.

"No, that's okay! The sooner I have his sermon behind me, the better I'll feel."

Together, they left the room and quietly crept into the kitchen. Mr. Bratton was still snoring loudly on the sofa.

"Oh, look, there's some tea already made." Crissy pointed at the glass teapot on the table.

"Great! But it's probably from last night. Does that matter to you?"

"Nah, as long as it's wet!"

Maggie put the teapot in the microwave and zapped it for a minute.

Hurriedly they drank two cups and ate some toast with jam. Afterwards, they went back to Maggie's room to get her saddle and tack.

"Can you carry my grooming bag?" asked Maggie, who was carrying her saddle on her arm.

"Sure! Do you need anything else?"

Maggie thought it over. "Can you get a few carrots? They're in the refrigerator, in the bottom, on the left-hand side. That would be great!"

"I'll be right back." Crissy disappeared, and while Maggie closed her door quietly, she heard a loud bang coming from the kitchen.

"Darn it!" Crissy exclaimed. When she had opened the

33

refrigerator, a half-full jar of jam had fallen out and shattered on the tiled floor. "What a mess!"

"What's going on?" came a sleepy-sounding voice from the living room.

"Oh, no, that's all we need." Maggie, who had joined Crissy in the kitchen, took a deep breath. "Here we go!"

The girls tried to prepare themselves for the storm they were sure was about to break from Mr. Bratton.

He stood in the kitchen doorway, wrinkled from his sleep, and looked at the sticky mess on the floor in front of him.

"Can't you be more quiet at breakfast?" he grumbled. "Good morning, Crissy. What are you doing here so early?"

Crissy who was holding her breath, gave Maggie a quick look.

"Good morning, Mr. Bratton. Did I wake you up? I'm so sorry. I'll clean this up right away! Maggie, where do you keep your paper towel?"

"I'll do it!" Maggie tried to push her way past her father.

"Oh, my daughter!" Now, suddenly, he seemed to remember who he could blame for the uncomfortable night on the sofa.

"Imagine what happened to me," he said, and his voice sounded dangerously calm. "I came home last night and actually found my wife in the kitchen, sitting on the floor. Ah, when I say kitchen, it was really a harness room. So, your mother was kneeling in coffee grounds and leather polish, cleaning your saddle. Don't you think that's funny?"

Maggie swallowed. "Dad, please hear –"

"Just a minute! I'm not finished yet! So, she's sitting there and cleaning your riding tack. I wouldn't have been

34

surprised if I'd opened the kitchen cupboard and found a horse inside! And I asked, very politely, what we were having for dinner, and she offered me a can of soup. Imagine that!"

Then his voice thundered. "Do we live in a stable? You spend all of your time in the riding hall, you don't do anything here at home, and then you let your mother clean your saddle tack! Not only that, I'm supposed to eat soup out of a can! Well, let me tell you, that's it! I've had enough! This weekend is the last time you're going to ride that horse! Then I'm getting rid of him! Maybe then you'll remember that there are other things in life besides stinking stables and dangerous and worthless horses! Now, clean up this mess on the floor! It's disgusting around here!"

If looks could kill, Maggie would have been dead.

Crissy stood next to her, as white as a ghost. She had never seen her friend's father like that.

"You ... you can't do that! Giaccomo isn't worthless *or* dangerous! Anyway, you said I could keep him if I win second place in the jumping event! You can't just have him killed! That's not right!" said Maggie, her voice quivering.

"Don't you dare tell me what I can and cannot do!" yelled Mr. Bratton. And he stomped out of the kitchen, furiously slamming the door behind him with a loud bang.

Tears ran down Maggie's cheeks as she knelt on the kitchen floor and with trembling hands wiped up the sticky mess.

"I hate him! I hate him so much! He ... he's so mean!"

In the next instant, Maggie's mother was standing in front of her in her nightgown. "That wasn't the plan," she said quietly, and took the rag out of Maggie's hand. "Quick, go!

35

He'll calm down. I'll clean this up! Go, you're already late. I hope you have a nice day, in spite of this disaster! Now, get going, fast, before he comes out of the bathroom."

"How is this going to be a good day? Giaccomo ... he wants to get rid of him! He wants to ... actually have him killed!" sobbed Maggie, and she was so upset she couldn't catch her breath.

"We'll see about that. It's not that easy! No vet would agree to helping him when the horse is in such good health. Don't worry about it. He's just upset. Come on, get going!" urged Mrs. Bratton, and she ushered the two girls out of the kitchen and to the front door.

Maggie gave her mother a light kiss on the cheek. "Thank you, Mom! What would I do without you?"

Crissy said good-bye hurriedly, too. "'Bye, Mrs. Bratton. I'm so sorry!"

"You don't have anything to be sorry about. Now get out of here!" Maggie's mother even managed to smile and wave them off, until they had disappeared around the corner. Then she took a deep breath, closed the front door, and returned to the kitchen to wash the floor. Meanwhile her husband was still locked in the bathroom.

Vera Bratton looked at her trembling hands. She knew her husband, and knew that she didn't stand a chance of changing his mind while he was still angry.

*

"Our sweeties look great today, don't you think?" Ricki had taken a step backward and was carefully examining her magnificent black horse.

"Yeah, unlike us. We have black rings under our eyes and totally wrinkly faces," added Lillian, completely exhausted.

"If you two will just make up your minds about who wins the beauty contest, we can get going. We have to be at the riding arena in one hour!" Kevin, who had just arrived, pointed urgently to the large clock on the wall above the entrance to the tack room.

"Kevin, don't make us frantic. It's bad for our complexion!" grinned Cathy as she tightened Rashid's girth.

"If that happens, I'll apply a cucumber mask tonight, but we have to go – now! We shouldn't keep Crissy and Maggie waiting. After all, it's not only about the orphanage, it's also about Giaccomo!"

That worked.

Hurriedly, they put the finishing touches on their horses before they led them outside and mounted.

"I wish us luck," said Ricki as they rode off, and each of her friends knew exactly what she meant.

Chapter 3

Ten minutes after Crissy's phone call to Vince, the riding instructor, he had picked up both girls, including their saddles and tack and the poster, and was now heading toward the show grounds.

He'd noticed Maggie's red-rimmed eyes, but, seeing Crissy's warning glance, he avoided talking to the teenager about it. He imagined that Mr. Bratton was the reason for her being upset. Swearing him to secrecy, Crissy had told him about Mr. Bratton's threats concerning Giaccomo.

He tried to cheer up Maggie with funny anecdotes about some of his riding experiences, but was unsuccessful, and he was relieved when they finally arrived at the riding academy's parking lot.

"Do you have everything?" he asked, after the girls had removed their things from the rear of his old SUV and he had helped them carry the heavy saddles into the stable. Crissy headed straight for Evening Star's stall.

"Anything else I can do for you?" he asked Maggie.

Maggie shrugged her shoulders. "Just pray that

Giaccomo won't come to any harm," she whispered hoarsely as she opened the stall door and wrapped her arms around her horse's neck. She didn't know how she was going to survive this day, much less participate in the jumping event tomorrow.

Vince felt himself becoming furious at Maggie's father. "Don't worry," he replied quietly, and turned away. If it was at all possible, he was going to try to talk with Maggie's father.

Bratton has to be made to understand that he's destroying his daughter's spirit and self-confidence with his threats to destroy her wonderful horse, thought Vince as he left the stable and walked over to the registration table. The first participants were already standing there waiting for their placement assignments.

*

Ricki and her friends arrived at the riding show grounds to find that Crissy and Maggie had already placed their poster next to the table where Anne and Tyler were collecting the entry fees.

"Hi everybody!" called Ricki as she brought Diablo to a halt so that she could get a better look at the poster.

"That turned out really great!" commented Kevin, nodding his admiration.

"It looks like a really professional job! Which one of you painted it?" Cathy wanted to know.

"Who do you think? Not me, with my two left hands!" Crissy tied the poster to the table legs with string so that it couldn't fall over.

Maggie stood a few yards from them and stared with glazed eyes into the distance.

"Hey, Maggie, cheer up! We're going to show your father what a wonderful horse Giaccomo is!" Kevin called encouragingly to the girl. But she just turned and ran back into the stable.

"Did I say something wrong?" asked Kevin, unsure of himself.

Crissy just shrugged her shoulders. "No, it's just that I think anything you say to Maggie about Giaccomo and her father is going to upset her. This morning Mr. Bratton really flipped out. He was incredibly furious and he more or less decided that the horse would be put down after the show no matter what. Maggie's nerves are completely shot."

Depressed and upset, the friends looked at each other with long faces, and Ricki had a sick feeling in her stomach.

"He's crazy! He can't do that to a healthy, gentle horse like Giaccomo. It's inhumane!" she steamed.

"It's insanity! Absolute insanity! And under these conditions, we're supposed to have a kids' riding ring? Well, no way, you guys. I just can't do this. Can you?" Lillian had dismounted and was now leaning against Holli for support, fuming with anger.

"I feel the same way," Cathy agreed softly as she wiped a few tears from her eyes.

"I know this may sound dumb right now," began Kevin, "but we can't just pack up and go home. It wouldn't be fair to the kids at the orphanage. After all, we planned this event to help *them*."

"But they don't know anything about this," said Lillian. "If we don't do this kids' riding thing, everything will be exactly the way it was before."

"And if we do it, we'll be helping them for sure, and some good will come out of this awful situation!" argued Kevin with conviction. "And anyway, what else would we do? Stand around here for two days and cry about Giaccomo? That's not going to help us or Maggie or the horse. On the contrary. We're making ourselves crazier every minute we spend thinking about it. The kids' riding event could show Maggie's father that Giaccomo is a terrific horse, and that even little kids can ride him safely. Don't forget about that."

The girls nodded, dejectedly.

"Okay then, I guess you're right," said Ricki, and she took a deep breath before turning to Anne and Tyler, who had sat quietly by and listened to the whole thing. "If anyone asks about the Kids Ride for Kids event, please tell them that we'll start at nine o'clock. We'll ride around in a ring outside the exercise area."

"That's a pretty large ring," commented Anne. "You're going to be working hard for just one dollar."

"Hmm, that's true, actually," said Ricki as she surveyed the grounds.

"Maybe we could have the ring around the main tent," Cathy suggested.

"That's a good idea. That's where most of the people are. That's sure to raise more money." Lillian nodded in agreement.

"Okay, then. At the tent," Ricki decided. "Maybe you could tell people with kids here at the entrance about us."

41

"Sure, we'll do that." Tyler turned to greet some new visitors. "Good morning! How many people? Two adults, three children? Would you like your children to participate in the Kids Ride for Kids event?"

"Is there a riding event for children?" asked the woman, surprised.

"It's a new event we've organized to benefit the children at the local orphanage," Tyler explained. "You can read all about it on the poster."

"Well, I think it's a terrific idea. Activities of that kind deserve our support." The man nodded and the children were already jumping around their parents in anticipation.

"Oh, yeah, me first!"

"No, me!"

"Mommy, can't I be first? I'm the oldest."

The three children started to bicker loudly.

"If you all aren't a little quieter, none of you can ride! You're making the horses nervous," the father warned, and the noisy bunch quickly became quiet for fear that they wouldn't be allowed to ride at all.

"Good. Now, come on. First, we're going to look around for a while."

"The children's rides will start at nine o'clock at the main tent," called Tyler after them, and the woman thanked him with a wave.

"You're really good at that! Keep it up!" Crissy beamed. Then she saw her riding instructor at a distance and ran over to him.

"Hey, Vince, wait up a minute." When she caught up to him, she asked, "When you make the announcements on the loudspeaker, could you please mention our Kids Ride for Kids event? We're going to begin at nine o'clock at the main tent." She stood still, a little out of breath.

"Take it easy and catch your breath. I was going to mention the children's event anyway."

"Great! See you later." Crissy returned to the others, and Vince disappeared into the judges' stand.

*

Vera Bratton had used all her patience and powers of persuasion to talk to her husband after he had calmed down a little. She tried again and again to talk him out of his outrageous plan, but it was like talking to a stone wall.

Finally, after Maggie's father had made several attempts to get away from his wife's pleading, the otherwise good-natured and loving woman lost her temper. She stamped her foot in fury. "Really, Larry! Stop acting like a three-year-old child! The least I should be able to expect from an adult man, let alone my husband, is that he listens to what I'm saying and doesn't keep running away!" She looked at him threateningly, but he continued to ignore her.

"All right! Enough! As far as I'm concerned, you can keep on acting like a stubborn mule! If you want to keep pacing the apartment, don't let me stop you. But I guarantee you, I will keep following you until you listen to what I have to say!" Angrily, she pounded the dining room table with her fists, and the glass plates began to clatter ominously.

"Do you think that I don't know what's going on here? No? All right, then, I'll tell you! Giaccomo is just a side issue in this ridiculous game, but it's one that gives you leverage to use on your daughter." Her husband tried once

43

again to leave the room, but Mrs. Bratton stood in the doorway, blocking his escape.

"Yes, that's exactly what's going on," she continued. "Your real problem is not the horse. You've decided he's dangerous, although in truth he's as gentle as a lamb, or we wouldn't have bought him for our daughter. And it doesn't matter to you if he wins prizes at horse shows ... No! The only thing that bothers you is the fact that Maggie, at fifteen, is no longer a child! You seem to ignore the fact that in a few years she'll be an adult. Larry, she isn't your little girl anymore. She's a teenager who is about to become independent of her parents. Suddenly, her friends are more important than Mommy and Daddy, and when she pays more attention to her horse than to us, that's a sign that she's becoming a grown-up and learning to accept responsibly."

Mr. Bratton stood glaring at his wife, but she was determined that he hear the truth. "You just can't accept the fact that you are no longer number one in your daughter's life. Don't you see what you're doing? You're jealous of everyone and everything that stands between you and your daughter. Even if it's a horse! And you don't even realize that you're the one who's excluding yourself from Maggie's life! Do you really think your daughter will love and respect you if you threaten to have her horse put down? What do you expect to accomplish with that? That she'll wrap her arms around your neck? Larry, you're on the verge of ruining everything between you and Maggie."

Vera Bratton paused a minute and waited for her husband's reaction, but he just stared past her.

"Just pull yourself together and say something! It's easy to say nothing! Or is that all –"

Larry Bratton took a deep breath. "Vera, that horse is dangerous," he said with quiet intensity.

"Nonsense! That's ridiculous! Even I would have no anxiety about getting on Giaccomo, though I have no idea how to ride! Do you think Maggie would let little children ride him if she didn't trust him absolutely?"

Larry Bratton was silent. He knew his wife was right about everything she'd accused him of. But could he admit it? And as far as his feelings about Giaccomo were concerned, he was genuinely frightened for Maggie. Horses are unpredictable animals, always a risk. How could he have allowed this to happen? Why had he granted Maggie's wish for her own horse?

"How about this ..." offered Vera Bratton. "Let's go to the horse show around noon and see how the children's riding ring is going. I'm sure you'll see that your fears about Giaccomo are completely unfounded. And tell your daughter finally why you've been acting this way. I'm sure that she'll understand the real reason. Larry, it's not a crime to love your child, and certainly not to tell her so once in a while! But to have an innocent animal killed because you're jealous of it is inexcusable, and it will make Maggie pull away from you forever. And not just Maggie, do you hear me? I could never, never forgive you for that."

"Are you finished?"

"Yes!"

"Then leave me alone for a while! I have to think about everything you've accused me of!" he said brusquely,

"Good!" replied Vera. "You've got all the time in the world to think about this. Well, almost. I'm going to drive over to the riding academy about eleven-thirty. If you really

45

care about your daughter's love, you'll come with me."
Then she quietly left the room.

*

After Crissy managed to reassure Maggie that it wouldn't
be easy for her father to find someone who'd be willing to
put Giaccomo down, the girl calmed down some, and then,
with a heavy heart, she finally saddled her horse.

"You'll see, it will all work out!" Ricki was upbeat as
they brought their horses to the main tent.

The day was becoming unseasonably hot for early fall,
so the friends decided to divide the event into morning and
afternoon sessions and to use three of their horses for each.

Diablo, Holli, and Giaccomo would be the first ones to
carry the enthusiastic children around on their backs, and
Sharazan, Rashid, and Evening Star would do the afternoon
event.

Ricki and Lillian stood proudly beside their immaculately
groomed horses, but Maggie was still uneasy. She kept
glancing over her shoulder, always on the alert, afraid that
someone would come and take her horse away.

Giaccomo shone in the sun like polished oak, every bit as
handsome as the other horses.

The first customers were already milling around the
horses, full of admiration and curiosity. The girls, who
stood by proudly with glowing eyes, held the reins of their
beloved horses in their hands, and were almost embarrassed by the compliments of the people around them.
They were anxious for the first kids who wanted to ride to
arrive.

Suddenly Crissy came running up. "We are so stupid! Do you know what we forgot? We forgot to bring change! What are we going to do now?"

The friends looked at each other, perplexed. Everything was so well planned, but they had completely forgotten about the need for change.

"Hi, everybody! Well, how's everything going?" Mrs. Marshall had come at just the right time.

"Mom, thank heavens!" said Crissy. "You got here just in time. Can you help us? We –"

" – forgot the change," Crissy's mother completed her daughter's sentence, as Crissy stared at her in disbelief.

"How did you know that?"

Mrs. Marshall laughed. "I knew, because you never mentioned anything about getting change together when you were telling me about all of your preparations and plans. Usually, when you want to charge for something you're planning, you always ask me to get you change for bills. This time you didn't, so I thought I'd bring it with me just to be on the safe side. So here's a fanny pack with fifty one-dollar bills in it!"

"Mom, you're the greatest!" Crissy beamed like a lit-up Christmas tree.

Just then, a large group of children arrived.

"Is the kid's riding ring here?"

"Wow, that horse is pitch black!"

"Do you have ponies, too?"

"Can you just ride on the horses?"

"Ohh, you have to wait so long!"

"What? On all three? Great!"

"I want to go around six times!"

47

"Are you nuts? Then the rest of us will *never* get a turn!"

The little kids all shouted at once, until finally three of them were sitting in the saddles.

While Diablo and Holli stayed completely calm, Giaccomo's ears moved back and forth nervously, but this had more to do with his upset owner than with the small child sitting on his back.

"Stay calm, Giaccomo, they're just kids! They won't hurt you. They just want to sit on your back." Maggie patted his neck, soothingly, and then led him close behind Holli, who was following Diablo.

"So, what's your name?" Maggie asked the little boy who clenched Giaccomo's mane tightly in his hands and kept raising his knees, trying to look like a jockey.

"Mike! Wow, this is really high!" he said.

"Stay relaxed, nothing will happen to you, I promise. Anyway, it's much more comfortable if you let your legs hang down," advised Maggie, but her advice didn't help at all. The little boy was scared to death, but he tried to hide it. When his round was over, he slid slowly out of the saddle, and once he felt the ground beneath his feet, he started to brag a little.

"Hah, riding is really easy. Anybody who's afraid of this is just a scaredy-cat!"

"Do you want to go again?" asked Maggie, amused, as she noticed that she was calming down a bit.

"Ah, maybe not. You know what, my stomach is hurting a lot!" the boy said, and then he ran off.

The others laughed, and the next child was soon in the saddle.

The two girls, who were so happy sitting on Holli and

Diablo, spent the whole time thinking about how they could persuade their parents to pay for some more rounds.

"You know what," one of them said. "If Mommy won't pay for it, I'm going to go home and get my allowance!"

"You're lucky," the other one said. "I don't have much left of my allowance right now. I bought a book last week –" and so it went.

Lots of kids stood in line, and many of them had already ridden a few times. They'd already figured out how to stand in order to get up onto the horses.

Maggie threw Crissy, who was collecting the money, a knowing look. She was sure they'd be seeing see one or more of these kids taking lessons at the riding academy soon.

"Hey, Maggie, this is really going well, don't you think?" Lillian called to her.

"Great!" nodded her friend, and Ricki gave a thumbs-up sign. Smiling, she looked around at the children who were waiting for their turn to ride, and noticed a little boy standing at a distance with his father.

"I want to ride, too! Daddy, you promised me!" Billy kept tugging on his father's sleeve and then pulled him over to the horses.

Alex Berger sighed. In spite of the promise that he had made at the entrance, after seeing the poster, now that he was standing so close to the big animals he had some reservations.

"Would you like to ride Diablo?" Ricki asked the little boy pleasantly, and bent down to his level.

Embarrassed, Billy shook his head.

"I want to ride that one over there!" Determined, he pointed to Giaccomo.

"So, you really want to get up on that huge brown horse?" asked Alex, to make sure.

Billy nodded excitedly.

Ricki had to laugh when she saw the skeptical look in the father's eyes.

"Don't worry! Giaccomo is large, but he's incredibly gentle. See for yourself." She pointed to Maggie, who was just lifting a three-year-old into the saddle, and then swung up behind him. She guided Giaccomo with one hand, and with the other she held onto the little boy, whose face was beaming.

The gelding knew the way by heart and placed one foot calmly in front of the other, as though he understood he had to be especially careful because of the child.

Alex nodded. "I see, I've been overruled! Okay, one round for Billy," he said, and tried to pay Crissy.

"Ooooh, Daddy, I don't want to ride just one time! Look, the sign says 'Six rides for five dollars.' It's cheaper that way! Please, please!"

Alex gave in and handed the girl five dollars.

"Yippee!" shouted Billy, and scared Holli, who was just walking past him, but Lillian had her horse firmly under control so that nothing happened.

"Please, be a little more quiet when the horses are walking by," she told the kids. "When you're around horses you have to be very calm, because if you're nervous, you'll make the horses nervous, and we don't want that, do we?"

The children listened intently, and they were completely quiet now in the line.

Holli had just become available, and Lillian wanted to lift Billy up into the saddle, when the little boy protested loudly.

"I want to ride on the brown horse!" A little embarrassed, he stared at Lillian.

"Oh! Well, my horse will be glad to rest for one round!" she laughed, and sent the boy over to Maggie.

"Oh, please!" A redheaded little girl tugged at Lillian's sleeve. "I like this horse! I've always wanted to ride a white one! In all the movies, the princess sits on a white horse! And I'm a princess!"

"Wonderful! Well, here we go, your majesty!" grinned Lillian, sitting her securely in the saddle, and starting off again with Holli.

In the meantime, the first rush of kids was over and Billy was able to take his six rounds all at once.

"I could sit here like this forever," he commented with a dreamy look in his eyes, and Maggie understood what he meant. She felt exactly the same when she rode Giaccomo.

"Does this horse belong to you?" asked Billy, as she lifted him out of the saddle.

"Yes, it was a birthday present from my parents," Maggie answered, and was immediately reminded of her father.

Billy looked up in disbelief. "Is that for real? I mean, that you can get a horse for your birthday?"

"Yes, but I think it's unusual," said Maggie, a little depressed, but then she pushed her negative thoughts aside. The next child was already waiting for a ride.

She smiled once more at Billy, and then she started the next round, as the little boy gazed longingly at Giaccomo.

"Well, was it fun?" asked Alex, as Billy jumped into his arms.

"Yes, Daddy, it was great! Can I go again? Please, please, please."

"Oh, come on, Billy, you've been riding long enough!"

"But, Daddy, the woman at the entrance said that this is for a good cause. For an orphanage, I think. Daddy, what's an orphanage?"

Oh, no! thought Alex. How was he supposed to explain that to his son without opening up the old wound of the loss of his mother about a year ago?

As Alex was formulating his answer, an older woman, who was standing nearby and had overheard Billy's question, gave him an unrequested, and unwanted, response.

"An orphanage is a house where children without parents grow up. If the parents don't take care of them or if they die, many children go into an orphanage. But you don't have to worry, little boy. With such a loving father, I'm sure you have a nice mommy, too, and I'm sure that they won't take you to an orphanage."

Billy's eyes filled with tears, and his facial expression, so happy a moment ago, was now one of sadness.

Alex hugged him close and looked angrily at the woman.

"You shouldn't have said anything! I'm perfectly capable of answering my son's questions myself! Even though you certainly didn't mean to be cruel, you have no idea what your words have done to him. The boy lost his mother a while ago and today was the first day that I have seen him laughing again, until you –"

The woman turned pale. "Oh, no, I am so sorry. Please excuse me, I didn't know. I work at an orphanage, and I was so delighted that finally someone has done something to help those poor children. In my enthusiasm, I just answered without thinking. I was hoping that some people would hear me and become more aware of the fate of these children, and maybe donate a little money! I had no idea that your boy had lost his mother. Please forgive me!"

Alex swallowed, but then he nodded to her and turned away with Billy.

"I want to go home," whispered Billy, tears running down his cheeks.

"Okay, come on." Alex lifted him up on his shoulders and started to leave with him, when Maggie, who had just dismounted from her last round, saw the boy crying.

"Hey," she called over to him. "The ride wasn't that bad, was it?"

Billy stared at her and then turned his head away silently.

Maggie glanced at Crissy questioningly, and she explained what had happened.

Spontaneously, Maggie swung herself back into the saddle and called to Ricki and Lillian, "I'll be right back! Can you guys keep going without me for a while?" Then she steered Giaccomo straight toward Alex and Billy, until she was blocking their path.

Startled, Billy jumped when he saw the huge horse in front of him.

Alex looked quizzically at Maggie, and the girl nodded to him, almost imperceptibly, before she spoke to the little boy, pretending to joke with him, but also being sympathetic.

"Hey, Billy, I have a little problem. Maybe you could help me with it. I want to go get something to drink for me and my girlfriends, but it's so hard to ride and hold drinks at the same time. Would you please ride over to the drink stand with me? You were so good in the saddle back there, and I don't think Giaccomo would mind if we both sat in the saddle together. He likes you!"

As though he had understood, the horse lowered his magnificent head and poked Billy with his velvety nose, as if to say, *Hey, would you like to be my friend*?

Billy was still crying, but he couldn't resist Giaccomo's charm and threw his arms around his neck.

Maggie waited, without saying anything, and Alex stayed calm, too. He sensed that the girl just wanted to help.

"Well, do you want to?" Maggie asked, but Billy turned away, shook his head, and walked slowly away.

Alex shrugged his shoulders in resignation and said softly, "Thank you very much for trying to help. That was really nice of you."

Maggie nodded sadly but then her eyes looked determined.

I'll get him yet! she thought, and steered Giaccomo over to the boy again. Without paying any attention to Alex, she rode so close to Billy that the horse almost touched him.

Billy looked back over his shoulder and began to run, to show them that he wanted to be left alone. But Giaccomo stayed close to his heels until the little boy stopped and turned around angrily.

"Can't you two leave me alone?" he shouted so loudly that Giaccomo jerked backward nervously. Billy's screams weren't really about Maggie or her horse. In truth, he was just shouting to get rid of his sadness.

Now the people standing around him began to notice, and several angry glances were fixed on Maggie.

"What's she doing to that poor kid?"

"Look at that, he's really scared of the horse!"

"She must be crazy to ride after him like that!"

"That's enough!" Maggie felt her anger rising. She turned around and steered Giaccomo toward the bystanders. Her eyes sparkled angrily and her voice shook with fury.

"Mind your own business! You have no idea what's going on here! It's so typical – everyone has an opinion without knowing anything! The boy knows that this horse is as gentle as a lamb. Do you have any idea what I'm doing? No! All you see is a crazy girl on a mean horse, chasing a child and making him cry. You don't see anything else. How could you? You didn't see how happy he was fifteen minutes ago when he was sitting in the saddle. Why don't you just leave us alone?"

Giaccomo lowered his head again toward Billy, who had approached the horse without Maggie noticing.

"That horse is about to bite you! Hey, kid, look out!" shouted a hysterical voice from somewhere in the crowd.

Giaccomo jerked back, frightened, and would have taken a giant step forward if Billy hadn't been standing there. The boy laid his arm around the horse's neck and gave him a big kiss. Then he looked up at Maggie, who was completely surprised, and asked her quietly, "Will you help me up?"

For a moment, the girl wasn't capable of moving, but then she reached down to the child and pulled him up into the saddle. She had tears in her eyes, as Billy yelled to the crowd, "This horse doesn't bite! He is the nicest horse in the world, and that –" he pointed to Maggie – "that's my friend!"

Maggie swallowed hard, hugged the boy tightly, and

55

gave him a kiss on his tousled head. Then she turned Giaccomo and rode off toward the drink stand.

Alex and Crissy, who had hurried over, looked at each other. Amazed, the man watched his son ride off.

Crissy was proud of her girlfriend, who was always direct and honest and said what she meant.

"Don't worry, those two will be right back," she said to Alex, but she wasn't sure he'd even heard her.

Chapter 4

Vera Bratton was putting on her shoes when she sensed that her husband was standing behind her. She held her breath and waited for him to speak.

"Um, Vera, I ... I think you may be right. I have been acting badly," he said in an even toned voice. "What I need to do is help Maggie grow up, not keep on treating her like a child."

Vera smiled and breathed a sigh of relief. *I made it, I got through to him!* She rejoiced inwardly. "I'm glad you've come to realize that. Now, are you going to come with me to the horse show? I think it would be good for you to talk to your daughter."

Larry nodded, and without another word, the couple left the house.

*

Crissy came running back to her friends as Lillian was talking with Ricki. "Do you know where Maggie is? She seems to have disappeared, and now we're working ourselves to death here," exclaimed Lillian.

"Calm down, she'll be back soon. Maybe she had to make a pit stop," grinned Ricki, winking.

"With Giaccomo? How's she going to fit him in the Porta-Potty? Hey, Crissy, where's your girlfriend? Doesn't she feel like doing this anymore?"

Crissy shook her head energetically and told them what had just happened.

"Wow! I didn't know Maggie was so good with kids. She'll make a terrific child psychologist," commented Lillian, no longer angry.

"I could imagine her doing that. Hey, when are we going to take a break? My brain is absolutely fried. Anyway, business is slowing down. It looks like we've already taken most of the kids here for a ride," Ricki announced.

"Well, it's almost lunchtime, and most people are probably getting something to eat. I wouldn't mind eating something myself. Why don't we stop for now and start up again after lunch, around two o'clock? Lots of new visitors will be coming this afternoon." Lillian stretched her aching back.

"Exactly, and then it's Evening Star, Sharazan, and Rashid's turn! Where are Kevin and Cathy?" asked Ricki, who hadn't seen her two friends for quite a while.

"I think they're near the dressage grounds," said Crissy. But then she spotted them coming from another direction. "There they are."

"Hey, you guys missed the best part of the whole horse show!" exclaimed Kevin from a distance. Cathy, at his side, excitedly nodded in agreement.

"Did you know that they had organized trick-riding exhibitions with costumed Cossack riders? Man, that was awesome! Just the idea of straddling two horses and then, while they're galloping, doing acrobatics, makes me dizzy! How'd you guys make out? Did you have a lot of kids?"

Ricki nodded. "Well, I don't need to stand up on Diablo to get dizzy. The sun did the trick, but you two can find that out this afternoon."

"I'm sure!" Kevin grinned. "Are you guys taking a break now?"

Lillian looked at her watch. "Let's keep going for another thirty minutes. By then it'll be noon and our three-hour stint will be over. Crissy, how heavy is your fanny pack? How much do you think we earned?"

Crissy shrugged her shoulders. "I have no idea. We can count it later."

"Can I have a ride?" a little girl asked them just then, as she tugged on Lillian's T-shirt.

"Of course. One ride?"

The little girl nodded and gave Crissy a dollar, and then Kevin lifted her up and onto Holli's saddle.

"Hold on tight, here we go!" announced Lillian, and she started to lead Holli at a slow pace.

*

Maggie guided Giaccomo carefully past the visitors, trying desperately to find the right words to comfort the little boy who sat in front of her, sharing the saddle. But before she could say anything, Billy began to talk.

"Mommy was always so good to me, and I miss her so much. Daddy told me that she was very sick – cancer, he called it – and that she wasn't ever coming back. Why did

59

she do it? Why did she get sick and die and leave us alone when she knew how much we loved and needed her?"

"You know, Billy, that's not easy to explain. People don't get to decide if they're going to get sick or stay healthy. I'm sure your Mommy would have preferred to be healthy and stay with you. I'm positive of that. You shouldn't be angry with her. She couldn't help it that she got sick and died. And look at it another way. Your Mommy probably suffered a lot when she was sick, and now she's at peace and not in pain anymore." Maggie paused to give Billy some time to think about what she had said.

For a while, they rode on in silence. They'd left the show grounds and were riding along a path that led to the woods.

"The beverage stand is really pretty far from the riding hall," commented Billy.

Maggie nodded slightly. "You know what, I wasn't really thirsty anyway," she admitted softly. "I could see that you were very sad, and I just thought, since you were so happy riding on Giaccomo, that well, I –"

"You wanted to do something to take my mind off my Mommy, didn't you?"

"That's right." Maggie felt uneasy. Billy, in a hostile, accusatory tone, had taken the words right out of her mouth.

"Please stop!" It sounded like a command. Maggie sighed. *I did something wrong*, she thought, and she brought Giaccomo to a standstill.

Billy turned his head around abruptly and looked at her with a strange expression in his eyes.

"You thought you could replace my Mommy with your horse? That I would just forget her when I sit in this stupid saddle? Let me down! I want my Daddy!" His eyes glis-

60

tening with tears and anger, he tried to wriggle out of her arms and slide out of the saddle.

"Let me go!" he shouted all of a sudden, this time scaring Giaccomo.

Maggie let Billy down to the ground just as the horse reared up on his hind legs.

"Giaccomo! No!" Maggie, who was sitting awkwardly in the saddle, lost her balance and flew out of the saddle in a high arc and landed on the path. Giaccomo, in fright, kept on going a few yards, while Billy, completely shocked, crouched on the ground.

Maggie groaned. Her face was contorted in pain and her right leg was twisted under her. "Ohhh ... That really hurts!" The pain brought tears to her eyes. She saw Billy out of the corner of her eye.

"Are you okay?" she panted. Her face turned pale gray.

The boy nodded, white as a ghost. "I'm sorry! It's all my fault! Please forgive me, I didn't want this to happen! I ... you ... oh, what happened to your leg?"

Maggie closed her eyes, let her head hang back for a moment, and took a deep breath. The pain was almost unbearable, and as soon as she opened her eyes, everything around her started to spin. She groaned out loud, and she could feel Billy's cold little hand on her forehead.

"Hey, please don't die! You're my friend! Please don't go away like Mommy! I really like you!"

When Maggie turned her head to the side, she looked straight into Billy's wide, frightened eyes.

"Come here, kid." Her voice shook a little, as she held herself up with one arm and pulled the boy to her with the other.

"I like you, too, really, or I wouldn't have followed you on my horse."

"Honest? And you're not ... mad at me? And ... and ... we're still friends?"

Maggie smiled through her pain. "Of course! But you have to promise me never to shout again when a horse in nearby! Oh, no, where's Giaccomo?"

Billy pointed off to the side. "He's in the meadow, grazing."

Maggie nodded, relieved. "Well, if he's eating, then he's okay. Now all we have to do is figure out how we can get back to the show grounds. Wait a minute, I'm going to try to stand up." With all her strength, she managed to get up, but then in the same instant she screamed and fell back down. The pain was too intense.

Once again, tears came to her eyes. *Just don't faint*, she told herself.

Giaccomo had come closer and was looking at his rider. Since when was he allowed to graze all alone in unknown meadows? Well, whatever, at least the grass tasted wonderful. Snorting, he buried his nose in the sweet-smelling grass and continued to graze happily.

"Do you think you could bring Giaccomo over here?" Maggie's voice sounded strained.

Without hesitation, Billy nodded and jumped up. He was glad that he could do something. He felt really bad about what had happened to Maggie.

"Sure! I'll do it! I'll be right back." Excited, he wanted to run straight over to the horse, but Maggie's voice held him back.

"Slowly, Billy! You have to coax him to come to you. Do

62

you have any sugar cubes with you? No? Then come here. I have one in my pocket." Trembling and sweaty, she handed the piece of sugar to Billy, who walked over to the horse, cautiously, with his hand stretched out and spoke to the horse in a gentle voice.

"Come here, boy. Look what I have for you, mmm, a really nice sugar cube, just for you. Come here, Giaccomo."

The horse looked at Billy and began walking toward him. While the horse noisily nibbled his reward, Billy grabbed the reins and tried to run back to Maggie. However, the brown horse stood still and refused to move forward. Cautiously, Billy pulled on the reins a little, but Giaccomo just raised his head a bit and remained as still as a statue.

"He doesn't want to come! What should I do?" Billy's voice sounded desperate.

"You'll have to be more firm with him." Maggie could only whisper, and Billy didn't understand what she said, but he seemed to guess what she meant, and pulled the reins a little harder.

Suddenly, the horse whinnied shrilly, and turned his head toward Maggie, who fell over and remained still.

"No!" Billy screamed, let Giaccomo go, and ran back to Maggie. "What's wrong with you? Why don't you say something?" Billy was horrified.

Frantically, he looked around, but he couldn't find anyone, and the riding academy was too far away for anyone to have heard his shouts.

He looked at Maggie once more. Then he swallowed hard and turned around, determined. Slowly he approached the brown horse, which came toward him and allowed him to grab his reins.

63

Billy looked all around. About twenty yards away, there was a pile of stacked logs at the edge of the woods. The boy led the horse there, placed him parallel to the logs, and then, with a huge effort, used the logs to climb into the saddle.

Giaccomo stood still and stayed calm. He began to walk only when he realized that the boy was sitting in the saddle. Very slowly and carefully, he walked forward, as though he understood that the boy in the saddle didn't know how to ride.

Carefully he made a circle around Maggie, who was lying on the ground, still not moving.

"I'm going for help! Please, please, don't die," Billy cried.

The boy held onto the saddle tightly, and the reins lay loosely around Giaccomo's neck. The horse walked straight back toward the show grounds.

*

Vera and Larry Bratton had arrived at the riding academy and were asking Vince where they could find their daughter, when Ricki signaled Lillian with her hand.

"That's it for me!" she called happily. She could hardly wait to get an ice-cold soda, which she planned to pour down her parched throat. But first she had to see to Diablo. Vince had arranged for four empty stalls in the boarding stable, where the four friends could rest their horses during the breaks.

Alex, somewhat worried, kept looking at his watch. Where was Maggie with his son? By now they'd been gone for forty-five minutes.

"If someone comes for a ride now, I'll tell them to come back later," Crissy said. "Your horses will be glad to get out of the sun."

Lillian nodded, and lifted a little girl, the last rider of the morning session, into the saddle.

"This is great! I'm going to come back this afternoon, too. My mommy promised me I could." Then the little girl was quiet, but just as Lillian was starting off with Holli, she pointed ahead with her finger.

"But this afternoon, I want to ride all by myself, like that boy over there. This morning he rode only one time on the brown horse, and now he gets to ride all by himself!"

"What?" Lillian stopped Doc Holliday. "Where?"

"Over there," said the girl, pointing. "See, he gets to ride all by himself! Can I, too?"

Lillian's gaze followed the little girl's hand. She turned pale. There was Giaccomo, with a young boy in the saddle. But where was Maggie?

Quickly, she pulled the little girl back down from the saddle, despite her protests. "You can have two rides for free this afternoon, but not right now! Something's wrong!" Lillian sprang into the saddle.

Crissy grinned at her from a distance and called out, "Hey, Lillian, how many turns are you going to have?"

"Something must have happened to Maggie! Giaccomo is coming back alone with the little boy! I'm going to go have a look!" yelled Lillian, and then she trotted past Ricki, who was completely baffled. *What's with her?* she asked herself as she watched Lillian disappear.

Crissy turned pale when she saw Giaccomo without Maggie. "Oh, no!" she whispered, frightened.

Alex had been watching Lillian's quick actions, and now he came running over to Crissy. "What's wrong? Has something happened to Billy?"

Crissy shook her head. "It looks like Billy is okay, but I don't know what's happened to Maggie. Lillian's gone to look for her!"

*

Lillian trotted rapidly toward Giaccomo, who stopped and greeted his fellow horse companionably. Holli stood absolutely still in front of him.

"What's happened to Maggie?" Lillian had to force herself not to scream at the little boy, who was holding onto the saddle for dear life.

"She's back there! She fell off her horse and her leg looks weird. And ... all of a sudden, she stopped moving and talking!"

"Maggie fell off her horse? Why? What happened?" Lillian held her breath.

"She ... I yelled, and scared Giaccomo!"

"Oh, no!" Lillian's voice shook with fear for her friend. *I just hope nothing has happened to her. Oh, no, and now what's going to happen to Giaccomo when her father finds out about this accident?* Lillian couldn't bear thinking about it.

"Honey, you need to ride back to the show grounds immediately. Somebody should call an ambulance right away. I'm going to find Maggie. Do you understand me?" Lillian didn't wait for Billy's answer, but just rode off on Holli as fast as possible.

66

Darn! I forgot to ask where Maggie is! I hope I find her! If I have to ride back, it'll take too long!

At first, Giaccomo wanted to run after Holli, but Billy's forceful, "No!" and his desperate tugging at the reins held him back.

Slowly, the horse trotted back to the show grounds, where Alex, Crissy, Ricki, and the others were waiting for him. Cathy and Kevin were nowhere in sight, but Vince, who had already been informed by Crissy that something was wrong, came running up just as Alex, with a worried look on his face, was lifting a sobbing Billy down from the saddle.

"Daddy, Daddy! Maggie is lying back there on the path, and she isn't moving anymore. She fell off her horse. I shouted and scared Giaccomo, and ... the girl rode to help her. The ambulance is supposed to come. Daddy, it's all my fault!"

"Calm down." Vince grabbed Billy by the shoulders, turned him around, and looked at him gravely. "Where exactly did all this happen?"

Billy sniffed. "Back there on the path! Before the woods. Please, she's going to be okay, isn't she?"

"I don't know, but the ambulance will get there very soon. When did it happen?"

Billy shrugged his shoulders. "I don't know, maybe twenty minutes ago? I don't have a watch!"

"And how come you just got here?"

"She wanted me to catch Giaccomo first, and when I got him, she stopped moving all of a sudden. Before that she told me that I should never yell when a horse is nearby, and that she's my friend!" Billy sobbed.

67

Vince turned away and ran straight toward the parking lot, where, fortunately, the ambulance had been parked all morning, just in case of accidents. He got in with the two paramedics, and the ambulance sped away.

Crissy held Giaccomo's reins tightly in her trembling hands. She was too upset to even take a step.

Ricki stood next to her with Diablo. Desperately she tried to find some comforting words for Crissy, who was scared to death for her friend.

To make matters worse, Billy was still crying loudly. "I feel sick, Daddy. It's my fault! Giaccomo is a really gentle horse. He brought me back here so carefully! Oh, Daddy, if only I hadn't –"

"Stop it, you can't change anything now! We'll just have to wait until the ambulance gets back. Then we'll know more." Lost in thought, Alex stroked his son's head.

Ricki wrapped her arms around Crissy and looked her straight in the eye. "Everything's going to be all right," she told her softly, and hoped that her words wouldn't turn out to be a lie.

"Hey, Crissy! What's wrong? How can you be in a bad mood on such a beautiful sunny day?" Vera Bratton greeted her daughter's friend happily, and even Larry tried to smile pleasantly when he saw Crissy. He was ashamed of his angry outburst that morning, which the girl had witnessed.

Crissy groaned and looked at Ricki desperately. "That's all we need!" she whispered hoarsely. "Now, now it's over! When Mr. Bratton finds out what's happened, then –"

Ricki understood at once what Crissy meant. Giaccomo! *We have to get him out of sight, now!* She tried to act normal as she mounted Diablo and reached out to Crissy for Giaccomo's reins.

"I'll take him back to his stall. I'll see you later, okay?" she said, trying to keep her voice steady.

"But I –" Crissy looked at her a little bewildered.

"I'll take him back to his stall, now!" Ricki repeated slowly and firmly, and she stared at Crissy with a pleading look that said, *Give me the reins*.

Ricki sensed that she didn't have any more time. When Alex found out that the couple were Maggie's parents, he'd feel obliged to tell them what had just happened.

"Just give me the reins!" Ricki whispered harshly to Crissy, who was lost in thought, and then she bent down from the saddle and grabbed them from the frightened girl. She urged Diablo on and pulled Giaccomo behind her, who followed unwillingly. She had a feeling that the life of Maggie's horse would soon be in jeopardy.

Ricki tried to get out of sight as quickly as possible and was heading toward the stable Suddenly, she pulled up short when she heard an angry voice.

"Where is that devil of a horse? I told you that beast was dangerous! Vera, let me go! I'll kill him myself! Where is Maggie?" Larry Bratton's voice almost cracked and he could be heard all over the show grounds.

Ricki felt cold chills run down her back. Trembling, she glanced at the horse she was leading. He certainly didn't understand that his fate was being decided. Maggie's father didn't know yet that she was leading Giaccomo. Because the horse was boarded out, Mr. Bratton had seen Giaccomo rarely in the few years since he and Vera bought him for Maggie, and as he didn't particularly care about horses.

69

They all looked alike to him. That fact was going to buy Ricki a little extra time.

Giaccomo can't go back to his stall ... Bratton will find him! That man is capable of anything just now, thought Ricki, frightened, and she tightened her grip on Giaccomo's reins.

Suddenly, she had an idea.

"Come on, Giacco! Come, come!" She urged Maggie's horse forward, and at the same time pressed her heels into Diablo's sides. Riding quickly around the side of the tent, she was glad to see that the brown horse stayed right beside Diablo.

After a few minutes they arrived at the stable, which was connected to the newly built riding hall. In addition to numerous interior stalls, which were all occupied, there were six outside stalls along the back of the long building – so-called emergency stalls for guest horses. These were empty at the moment and weren't filled with straw. The big advantage was that they weren't visible from the stable, or from the various entrances.

"You'll be safe here for a while," murmured Ricki to the brown horse. Quickly she knotted up Diablo's reins and led him into one of the unoccupied stalls so that he wouldn't wander away, and then she led Giaccomo into another stall and began to unsaddle him.

"I'm sorry, sweetie, but I have to close the upper part of the door so that no one sees you. Be good. I'll be right back and I'll bring you something to eat! Okay?"

Five minutes later, she rode Diablo to the main entrance of the stable and put him in one of the stalls Vince had reserved. After her horse was unsaddled and taken care of, she ran down the corridor and peered out of the door.

She was lucky that no one was nearby. The show was still going on, and the participating riders were either gathered around the dressage or jumping areas or they had already gone to lunch in the tent.

Since there was no one around, she loaded up the wheelbarrow with straw and hay and pushed it, as fast as she could, toward the outside stalls.

Giaccomo whinnied softly in his stall when he heard the squeaks of the wheelbarrow.

"Psst!" said Ricki, as she opened the stall door and rolled the ball of straw inside. "Don't make any noise, for heaven's sake!"

Quickly she spread out the straw in Giaccomo's hiding place and put a large portion of hay in front of his nose.

"That should do it, for a while. I'll be back tonight. You won't starve before then," she said quietly to the gelding, who snorted in her hair lovingly, but then he looked at her accusingly as she closed the double door completely.

Ricki quickly put Giaccomo's tack and saddle into the wheelbarrow and hurried back to the main stable. There she returned Maggie's gear to the tack room, where it belonged.

Out of breath, and with a pounding heart, she leaned against Diablo's stall and stared at him, relieved. For the moment, at least, she'd managed to keep Giaccomo away from the angry Mr. Bratton.

Chapter 5

She must be here someplace, thought Lillian as she galloped frantically down the road on Holli. *Over there!* "Maggie? ... Maggie! ... Whoa, Holli, stop!"

Lillian jumped down from the saddle, dropped the reins, and ran over to her girlfriend, who was lying motionless on the ground.

"Oh, my goodness, Maggie, say something!" Helpless, Lillian looked down at the ghostly pale girl, and then she grabbed her by the shoulders and began to shake her. "Wake up, Maggie! Maggie!"

"Oh, stop it!" Maggie began to groan softly. "I already hurt just about everywhere." Slowly she opened her eyes and gazed into Lillian's, which were opened wide with fear. "I thought you were giving the kids rides. What are you doing here?" Maggie tried to move, but the pain in her leg reminded her what had happened.

"Just lie still. The ambulance will be here any minute. I'm so glad you're awake!"

"What's happening with Giaccomo ... and with ... Billy?"

"Don't worry, they both turned up safe at the show grounds."

"That's great," Maggie said, exhausted, and she closed her eyes again.

"Well, finally!" Lillian said when she saw the ambulance speeding toward them. With a sigh of relief, she jumped up and danced back and forth wildly on the road, waving her arms to signal their location. When she was sure she'd been seen, she grabbed Holli and they stood about five yards from Maggie on the road.

The ambulance came to a stop, and Vince and the para-medics jumped out.

"How is she?" The riding instructor's concern showed in his face.

Lillian made a comforting gesture with her hand. "Well, at least her mouth still works! So I think she can't be that bad. She's already told me off for leaving my post at the children's riding event."

Vince heaved a sigh of relief, and the paramedics began to examine the injured girl on the ground.

"Ow! That hurts!" complained Maggie, as one of the paramedics began massaging her leg.

"We know, but there's no other way. We have to get your leg straight again. We'll give you something to relieve the pain before we put on a temporary splint. Then it's off to the hospital with you for an X-ray. I think that the bones will probably have to be set, and you'll have to have a cast, of course. I'm guessing you won't be doing any riding for a while!"

"That's just great!" Maggie grimaced with pain. "Everything's ruined, isn't it?"

"Well, for now, yes, but the doctors will be able to fix it. Don't worry!" The paramedics brought the gurney over, and together they lifted Maggie onto it.

*

Maggie didn't remember anything about the trip in the ambulance to the hospital, or about the operation to repair her broken leg.

Only after she came out of the anesthesia, and regained her memory of what had happened, did she realize what the consequences of the accident could mean for Giaccomo.

Fearfully, she glanced at her mother's worried face. Vera had stayed by her daughter's bedside the whole time, waiting for her to wake up.

"Mom, Giaccomo – " Maggie began, but Vera shook her head.

"Never mind Giaccomo for now. You mustn't upset yourself! You've had a concussion –"

"But when Dad –"

"Just stay calm and let me handle it. Nothing is going to happen to your horse!" Vera tried to appear relaxed, but inwardly, she wasn't really sure that she could guarantee Giaccomo's safety. Larry had been completely unnerved and almost out of his mind after Maggie's accident.

"Mom," said Maggie quietly. "If Dad does something to Giacco, then ... then I don't have a father anymore!" Feeling desperately afraid for her beloved gelding, she turned her head to the side, as tears ran down her cheeks.

*

After Larry Bratton heard from the surgeon that his daughter's operation was successful, he left the hospital hurriedly, without saying anything to Vera.

As he sat trembling behind the steering wheel in his parked car, he closed his eyes for a few seconds in order to think clearly. Now more determined than ever, he grabbed his cell phone, called Information, and got the numbers of the local vets. He was astonished and angered to discover that the first two he spoke with flatly refused to even discuss putting the horse down when they realized that the horse was neither old nor badly injured. Then some vague memory dawned on Mr. Bratton. There was one vet whose reputation was a bit … shady. There had been lots of rumors about him being involved in some illegal horse-trading. Mr. Bratton found his number on the list, dialed and waited impatiently for an answer.

"Dr. Pauley? This is Larry Bratton. I have a problem that can't be postponed any longer. I have this horse that I need to get rid of ...

Mr. Bratton explained and listened to the abrupt answer at the other end. What? Yes! I know this is Saturday, and, yes, I do know it's illegal. But I'm willing to pay you well ... what? That's outrageous! Okay, okay! Whatever! I'm willing to pay if you come and get the animal right away! Where? Oh, yeah. The riding academy in Avalon! What? Yeah, there's a show ... What do you mean, that doesn't make a good impression? Just say you're taking the horse in for treatment. His legs or something like that. It's nobody's business anyway! Good ... can I depend on you? Fine. Thanks a lot, Pauley. Good-bye!"

Slowly, he let the cell phone fall, and stared through the

windshield directly at the little sign attached to the rear window of the car parked in front of him:

Come to the grand-opening show of the Avalon Riding Academy and experience a whole weekend of lively events with your family! Dressage, jumping, exhibitions, contests, and plenty of good food await. Give yourself a treat and enjoy our beautiful, well-trained horses during this exciting two-day event. We guarantee a weekend you'll never forget!

"That's true, although for a completely different reason," mumbled Larry Bratton to himself, and turned the key in the ignition. He decided to drive over to the riding academy immediately to see to Giaccomo's transport. He had to be sure that the horse would be taken away before it could hurt his daughter any more.

*

Cathy, Kevin, and Crissy were sitting with Lillian and Vince at a table outside the main tent. Although they were a little relieved about Maggie, they all sensed the danger now hovering over Giaccomo. Larry Bratton had flown into an insane rage and had shouted so loudly in front of the tent that even the horses nearby had been frightened.

"There's nothing he could do that would surprise me," said Crissy quietly, more to herself than to the others.

"Where's Ricki? Didn't you say that she wanted to take Giaccomo to his stall?" asked Kevin, looking around.

"Oh, yikes, Ricki!" Crissy struck her forehead with her hand and then stood up. "Do you think we should go look

76

for her? I'm such an idiot! I just let her leave with the two horses instead of going with her to help unsaddle them and take care of them, but all I could think about was Maggie."

"We'll come with you!" responded Lillian and got up as well.

"Are you going to continue with the kids' riding this afternoon?" Vince wanted to know.

The friends looked at each other.

"Well, I guess we can't do anything about Maggie's accident anyway, and who would it help if we just stood around waiting? I think we should finish what we started. What do you guys think?" Lillian looked around at the others.

Kevin and Cathy nodded, but Crissy hesitated.

"Actually, I'd much rather go see Maggie, but she'll probably still be sleeping after the anesthesia. Okay, I'm in!"

"Terrific!" Vince swung his legs over the bench. "In case anything happens, I'll be in the judges' stand." He nodded good-bye and then walked off quickly.

Before the kids could go to the riding hall to look for their friend, Ricki came running toward them.

"How's Maggie?" she called to Lillian from a distance.

"She's in the hospital being operated on. Her leg was broken in a couple of places, and she had a mild concussion, but the doctors say she's going to be okay."

Ricki sighed with relief. "Well, she's young, and leg bones knit well! Thank heavens it wasn't anything more serious," she said, and she put her arm around her boyfriend and hugged him.

Kevin kissed her on the cheek. "Everything okay with Giaccomo?" he wanted to know.

Ricki nodded. "Yeah, I took –" she began, but was interrupted by the voice coming from the loudspeaker.

"And now, ladies and gentlemen, riding enthusiasts and show participants, we come to one of the high points of this weekend. Get ready to enjoy one of the greats in the international sport of dressage, the two-time national champion, Samantha Nolan!"

Lillian's head snapped around and her mouth dropped open when she heard the name of her all-time idol and role model.

"Samantha Nolan? Wow! Did you guys know she was going to be here today? Maybe even with Hadrian? I've always dreamed of seeing her in a live performance. Come on! We've gotta see this! She's amazing!" She grabbed Crissy's hand quickly and pulled her along.

"What's up with her?" grinned Cathy. "I've never seen our Lily like that before."

Ricki had to laugh, too. "True, but Samantha Nolan rides like a champion! You just have to see her! Come on, hurry, or all we'll be able to see are the heads of the people in front of us!"

*

After her daughter had dozed off again, Vera Bratton went to look for her husband. She guessed that he would be in the doctor's office, discussing Maggie's case. However, she couldn't find him, either in the corridor or in the office of the doctor on call.

"Mr. Bratton? I'm sorry, but he left about a half hour ago," the nurse who opened the door explained.

Maggie's mother turned pale. She had a sinking feeling she knew where he was. She thanked the nurse for the information and hurried off.

Out of breath from running, Vera Bratton arrived at the parking lot where just a short while ago her husband's car had been parked. She looked incredulous at the little blue sports car that was now parked in its place.

"He's really going to do it," she whispered to herself, shocked. She felt like she was going to faint. Taking a deep breath, she touched her hand to her cheek in horror.

Giaccomo! Oh, no!

As though in a trance, she ran back inside the hospital. "Please, I need a taxi! Could you get me one?" She almost screamed at the woman at the information desk.

"There' s a public phone back there," responded the receptionist brusquely, and she began to sort some hospital documents.

"I don't have any money with me! My handbag was in the car, and my husband has driven off! Please, call a taxi for me, before something awful happens!" In her desperation, Vera Bratton leaned in to the counter, as the shocked receptionist backed away.

"This phone is for hospital calls only!" the receptionist announced sternly, putting a protective hand on the receiver.

Vera looked up at the ceiling, and then she quickly reached through the opening in the glass window and grabbed the telephone from the receptionist's desk, pulling it toward her.

Determined, she dialed a number and stared at the hospital employee, who had turned white as a sheet.

79

"Don't worry! I'll be back and I'll pay for the call!" she snapped at her, and then she told the taxi dispatcher where she was.

She's crazy! thought the receptionist, as Vera slammed the receiver down on the hook and raced out of the building to wait for the taxi.

*

Tirelessly, Cathy, Kevin, and Crissy led their horses around and around the ring, and Lillian, who was collecting the money, noticed that the fanny pack was bulging.

"I think I'm going to have to empty this thing. It's so full, I doubt I'll be able to squeeze in another dollar bill," she grinned, patting the pack for emphasis.

"Take it into the club lounge," whispered Crissy. "No one will go in there. You can lock it in the cupboard and give Vince the key."

"That's a great idea, but how can I find Vince?"

"I think he's still in the judges' stand, taking notes on the performances."

Lillian nodded. "Okay! I'll be right back. Ricki, can you collect the money while I'm gone?" she asked her girlfriend.

"Of course!" Ricki nodded and she sat down at Lillian's place.

At just about the same time, the transporter driven by Dr. Pauley was slowing to a stop near the riding hall.

The driver left the van, a bad-tempered look on his face, and stomped toward the entrance. Astonished glances followed him.

"Well, this is just great!" he grumbled to himself. "This is not what I planned for my weekend. Having to pick up a horse during a horse show, just to have it put down! There really are some strange characters out there! It's a good thing no one knows why I'm here."

When he was in the stable corridor, he began looking around.

"Wouldn't you know it! No one's here! How am I supposed to know which horse it is?" In a bad mood, he reached into his pants pocket and pulled out a pack of cigarettes.

"You can't smoke in here," said a little girl dressed in a riding outfit. She had just entered the stable.

"Oh, really!" grinned Dr. Pauley. He was about to ignore her instruction, when he remembered his dilemma. "Hey, you," he began politely, as he let the pack slide back into his pocket, "where is that ... that – Wait a minute, I forgot the horse's name. Is it Jack, Jacko something?"

"Do you mean Giaccomo?" the little girl asked, trying to be helpful.

"That's it! Giaccomo! That's the one!" the man nodded assertively. "Which one is he?"

Remembering which stall Giaccomo was boarded in, she responded, "He's the one way in the back, next to the last stall on the right. Why are you looking for him?" The girl looked at the strange man, curious.

"I, well, I'm supposed –"

"Grace, where are you? You're up in twenty minutes! Have you got your horse saddled?" A somewhat bossy voice made the girl jump.

"Oh, I have to go! Keep your fingers crossed for me!"

81

The man grinned contemptuously. "Sure!"

"Thanks!" And the little girl disappeared.

Anything else? thought the man as he started walking down the stable corridor. Soon he stood in front of Giaccomo's stall and stared at the astonished gelding, shaking his head.

"Actually, you don't look as wild as the old guy on the phone said," he commented quietly and opened the sliding door. He looked the animal over and whistled admiringly. "Hmm, you're really too good to be put down, but what can I do? He's paying big money for this. Well, come on, let's get going!" He gripped the halter firmly and left the stall with the horse.

*

Lillian emptied the overflowing fanny pack and, as Crissy had advised her, locked the profits in the cupboard of the riding club's members' lounge. With the key in her hand, she whistled as she left the riding hall to look for Vince. Her glance wandered to the side and followed a transporter as it turned off the riding academy's property and onto the main road. She heard a horse neighing from the inside. Some vet's name was written on the side of the transporter. Had there been an accident? She wondered.

Then all of a sudden, a horrible suspicion struck her. Lillian turned and ran into the stable. Breathlessly she stopped short in front of Giaccomo's stall and stared in-credulously at the open sliding door.

"Giaccomo is gone," she whispered hoarsely. "That's why the van was here. That guy has actually taken him away! Oh, no!" In a blind panic, she turned around and ran out as quickly as her legs would carry her.

What should I do? Should I tell Crissy and the others? Or should I go to the show's directors? Or – A jumble of thoughts ran crazily through her head, and then she saw Vince approaching her.

"Well? Are you all finished with the kids' riding?" he called to her in a good mood.

"Giaccomo is gone! I'd just locked up the money in the clubroom cupboard and was coming to give you the key when I saw a trailer driving away with a horse on board. And Giaccomo's stall is empty!" Lillian's voice almost cracked as she grabbed the riding instructor's arm.

"Hey, have you been in the sun too long? What's wrong with you?" asked Vince, who couldn't understand anything from Lillian's rapid-fire outburst.

Lillian closed her eyes for a moment. *Stay calm,* she thought, and she pulled herself together and told Vince what had happened so that he finally understood.

"That's not true," answered the riding instructor, looking skeptically at Lillian. "That just can't be true."

"If you don't believe me then come and see for yourself! I told you, Giaccomo's stall is empty!"

Now Vince turned pale, too. Without another word, he ran off, with Lillian right behind him. Soon, they were standing in front of the vacant stall.

"The man is insane!" responded Vince, devastated. "Maggie will go crazy!"

"Isn't there anything we can do?" Lillian's eyes pleaded with Vince. "I mean, that's just not right, that he has his daughter's horse taken to be put down. Isn't that against

83

the law? Can't we just drive after the transport and get Giacco out?" Lillian brushed her long hair out of her face nervously.

"I'm afraid that won't help. If the owner ordered them to take him away, we can't do anything to stop it. Even though we suspect it, we can't prove that he took the horse to have him put down!"

"But Maggie is the owner! She didn't order anything to be done!" Lillian just couldn't believe it.

"But I ordered it! Maggie isn't eighteen yet, so I'm officially the owner. And as I see it, Dr. Pauley followed my instructions!" Larry Bratton suddenly appeared in the stable corridor and looked at the empty stall with satisfaction. "He took that wretched horse away, and what happens next is my business, not yours!"

Speechless, the two riders stared at Maggie's father, who had already turned to go.

"Just a minute!" Vince's sharp voice held him back. "You actually had Giaccomo taken away? How can you justify having a wonderful, healthy animal put down? Not to mention what you're doing to your daughter. You aren't even thinking about Maggie's feelings, are you?"

Larry Bratton glared at the riding instructor. "I don't think I have to justify myself to you, young man! But let me tell you that I was thinking *only* of Maggie! That horse would have killed her some day! He's a menace!"

"Giaccomo is one of the gentlest horses in the world. He wouldn't hurt a fly!" exploded Lillian, her voice shaking with anger.

"That's your opinion! All I can see is my daughter, lying in the hospital after that animal threw her off! That nag has to pay for that! Period!" Larry Bratton turned away – he wasn't about to let them keep him there any longer.

Lillian took a deep breath, and then she called after him, "That isn't it, Mr. Bratton! You know very well that every rider – experienced or not – falls off a horse some time or other, and usually it's the rider's own fault. For you this accident is just a welcome opportunity to get rid of Giaccomo! Do you expect Maggie to start spending more time with you again? That she'll throw her arms around you and say, 'Dad, you're the best!'? Mr. Bratton, Maggie is no longer the little girl who used to sit on your knee and think that you were the most wonderful man in the world." Lillian's voice broke.

Larry Bratton almost stumbled as he heard the teenager's words. He'd already heard those words once today. As tempted as he was to turn around and contradict her strongly, he decided against it and quickly left the stable.

"You did a good job, Lily," said Vince tonelessly, and he put his arms around the girl's shoulders. "I hope he'll remember what you said for a long time."

"But Giaccomo – Can't we maybe –?"

"I'm afraid not."

For a while the two were silent. Lillian sobbed quietly, and Vince had to work hard to keep from joining her. He couldn't bear to think about Maggie's reaction when she found out what had happened to her horse.

"We ... we have to tell the others," said Lillian finally, and they left the stable, feeling defeated.

Chapter 6

"Hey, where have you guys been? I was beginning to think maybe you'd run off with the money and were never coming back! Vince, did the other judges catch you red-handed?" called Ricki, grinning, as she saw Lillian and the riding instructor heading in her direction. When they got closer, the pleasure disappeared from her face. Ricki was startled to see her friend and the riding instructor approach with slow, measured steps and downcast eyes.

"What's the matter? You two look so blue," she asked. She turned to take the money for a ride from a little boy, and sent him over to Kevin and Sharazan.

Lillian and Vince looked at each other dejectedly.

"You tell them!" the girl pleaded.

"Giaccomo is gone!" Vince blurted out so loudly that everybody could hear.

"What?" Crissy rode over immediately on Evening Star.

"What do you mean, 'gone'?" Ricki asked. "That can't be. I put him –"

"Giaccomo's stall is empty. We just saw a vet transport van driving away, and Maggie's father was in the stable and con-

firmed that he'd had Giaccomo taken away by Dr. Pauley!"
Lillian's hands began to shake, and Ricki turned pale.

"No! That can't be! I –"

Crissy felt her legs begin to give way. Trembling, she leaned against her horse.

"That horrible bully! He really did it. Unbelievable! Oh, no, what's Maggie going to do when she finds out about this? Mr. Bratton must be completely insane! He –" The girl swallowed. It was a nightmare. Only a few hours earlier, Maggie had led the gentle Giaccomo, with a series of delighted children on his back, in a ring around the main tent without incident. Then came Billy, the motherless boy Maggie was trying to comfort.

Suddenly Crissy became furious with the little boy. It was his outburst that spooked Giaccomo, causing him to throw Maggie. Her injuries were bad enough, but the thought that the boy's careless behavior might result in Giaccomo's being destroyed was unbearable. It was his fault Maggie was in the hospital. And they had him to thank for Giaccomo being carted off to be killed.

In a fit of rage, she began yelling at the kids who were waiting patiently for their turn to ride the horses, "That's it! No more Kids Ride for Kids. If you kids don't know how to behave around these wonderful animals, you shouldn't be riding them. You're not getting any more rides on our horses ever again! I promise you that! Do you hear me? Get away from here, right now!"

Surprised and frightened by the girl's outburst, the kids broke the line and ran back to their parents for safety.

"Crissy, get a grip! I know you're upset – we all are – but have you lost your mind? You can't yell at those kids like

87

that. They had nothing to do with any of this. Don't take your anger out on them." Vince tried to reason with the girl, but Crissy ignored him and swung herself up into Evening Star's saddle.

"Oh, leave me alone! There's no telling what Maggie might do when she finds out what's happened! Do you hear me? Oh –" Abruptly she pressed her ankles into Evening Star's belly and trotted off.

*

Kevin had returned with Sharazan and the little boy from their round, and Cathy was just walking toward Lillian and Vince.

"What's going on?" she asked breathlessly. "Where's Crissy riding off to in such a hurry?"

"Giacco is gone! Lillian says that a van from Dr. Pauley's Animal Hospital came here and picked him up, and Crissy freaked out! I have no idea where she's going," answered Ricki, who, with an uneasy feeling, watched her ride away.

"That's not really true, is it?" asked Kevin, stunned by the news.

"Apparently it is. Hey, Kevin, ride after her and bring her back, will you?" pleaded Ricki. "She's totally freaked out."

"Okay!" Kevin jumped back into Sharazan's saddle and chased after Crissy. *That Bratton guy must be a total moron,* Kevin thought, *if he could do something like this to his daughter just to get revenge on a gentle horse.*

Once past the riding academy grounds the boy urged Sharazan into a full gallop to try to catch up with Crissy, but Evening Star was moving faster than he ever had before.

*

Vince spoke to the angry parents of the frightened children and tried to calm them down by explaining the situation that had sparked Crissy's blowup.

As he spoke, a short man with close-cropped hair and wire-framed glasses worked his way into the group. He listened intently to what Vince was saying, all the while fidgeting with a camera hanging around his neck.

"That's very interesting," he murmured, and focused on Ricki, who had been trying to say something, but Lillian and Vince just wouldn't listen to her. He was next to her in two giant steps.

"Excuse me," he began with a pleasant smile. "Those two have been telling a horror story! Don't tell me that it's all true!"

"Of course it's true! Does this sound like a fairy tale to you?" Cathy, who was standing beside Ricki, was furious.

"No need to get angry, young lady! My name is Peter Franklin, and I'm a reporter for the local newspaper. Here's my press badge. If what they're saying is true, then this would make a great human-interest story."

"No, it would definitely not! Publicity isn't going to help Maggie. She'd have a nervous breakdown for sure!" Firmly, Cathy shook her head no.

"Then it's true that the horse has been picked up and taken away! What was his name again?"

"Giaccomo! Are you satisfied now?" barked Cathy.

"Can I say something here?" Ricki had been nervously shifting her weight from one foot to the other the whole time. "Vince! Lillian! Everybody! Pleeeease!" she tried again.

"Just a minute, Ricki! Hold on," Vince cautioned.

"Not in a minute, *right now!* You have to come with me, *right now!* It's important!" Ignoring their objections, she grabbed Vince and Lillian and pulled them aside.

"Now listen! It's impossible for someone to have picked up Giaccomo! I didn't put him in his stall, and no one but me knew where he was!"

"What?" Vince shook Ricki hard. "Now you tell us? Where is he? I mean, where did you put ... why did you even ...?

"You guys wouldn't let me speak! Come on, let's go! I'm almost positive that Giacco is still where I put him!" Ricki ran off, and her friends, filled with new hope, followed her.

"Hmmm ... secret hiding places. This is getting better and better," grinned Peter Franklin as he followed the others, running and snapping photos at the same time.

Ricki ran around the riding-hall building and stopped short in front of the outside stalls.

"Here? Why did you put him in here?" asked Vince, perplexed, but he held his breath like the others, until Ricki, her fingers trembling, could open the latch. Giaccomo knocked the top portion of the door open with his muzzle, banging it against the wall of the stall. He whinnied loudly. It was an outrage to be locked in this stall for hours when the weather outside was so beautiful.

Speechless, Ricki's friends stared at the chestnut gelding and breathed a collective sigh of relief, while she rubbed the horse's forehead affectionately.

"Ricki, Maggie will be in your debt forever!" commented Lillian with admiration.

"We're not out of the woods yet. When Mr. Bratton finds

out about the switch, he won't stop looking until he's found the real Giaccomo," claimed Cathy.

Peter Franklin kept his eyes and ears open so that he wouldn't miss anything, and continued to snap photos.

"We should definitely get him away from here quickly. Maggie's father is sure to come back, and the last thing we want is for him to find Giaccomo!" Vince frowned as he thought about what to do. In his mind, he went through the list of his riding friends. Someone would be sure to have an empty stall where they could leave the horse, at least for the time being.

Suddenly Ricki snapped her fingers. "I have it! I can't believe I didn't think of it before!" she shouted and gave the astonished Giaccomo a big kiss right on his nose. "Giacco, boy, you're saved! When I get you to the stall I intended to put you in in the first place, no one will be able to find you, much less take you away! I promise!"

Lillian began to understand. "There's only one place for him to go!" she realized, nodding.

"Exactly!" agreed Cathy. Vince continued to look bewildered, and Peter Franklin was so curious that he forgot to snap any more photos.

"Well, I don't understand anything!" Vince said, exasperated. "Would someone please explain this to me?"

"Later, Vince! Later! I don't think it would be a great idea if a certain reporter found out where we're going to hide Giaccomo." Ricki stared straight at Peter Franklin, but he just grinned.

"I can be as silent as the grave," he replied solemnly.

"Yeah, sure you can!" Ricki's voice was heavy with sarcasm. "Oh, no, Mr. Franklin, you're not getting any more information from us!" With that, she turned away quickly. "I'll be right back. I'm going to get Giaccomo's and Diablo's snaffles, and then I'll take him away. Okay? Cathy, Rashid's still saddled. Can you come with me?"

"Of course."

"And what about me?" Lillian pouted.

"You should wait here until Kevin and Crissy get back, or they won't know what's happened or where we are."

"But Vince can do that, can't he?" Lillian looked pleadingly at the riding instructor, but he shook his head firmly.

"Sorry, Lily, but I should have been back in the judges' stand a long time ago! In spite of all of this, we do have a show today, and the show must go on, right?"

"Okay, I'll wait," sighed Lillian resignedly.

"Oh, stop sounding like a martyr. I'm sure they'll be back soon." With that, Ricki ran off to saddle Diablo.

"Come on, boy, stay still," she begged her horse as she laid the saddle across his back. "I'll be glad when we get Giaccomo away from here."

Diablo stared at her perplexed and poked her in the side, as though he expected his owner to give him an explanation.

"Oh, it's a long story," said Ricki laughing, and patted his neck. "Maybe Giaccomo can explain it to you in horse language!"

A few minutes later, the girl was riding around the stalls, and after Vince had attached the snaffle, Ricki took Giaccomo's reins and held them tightly, nodding good-bye to Lillian and the riding instructor. She trotted quickly down the narrow side road with Cathy at her side. After only a few yards, they disappeared into the woods. Ricki suggested that they ride in a zigzag pattern to confuse anyone who might be following them. She expected Peter Franklin to turn up at some point in hopes of discovering where they were taking Giaccomo. What the girls didn't know, however, was that the reporter had become so interested in a new story that was unfolding in front of the riding hall that he had completely abandoned his plan of following the two girls.

*

"Ricki is really the best, isn't she, Vince?" Lillian was just saying. "If she hadn't had the forethought to take Giacco to the guest stalls, tomorrow he'd have been – I can't even bear to think about it!" Relieved, she exhaled slowly and then took the riding instructor's arm.

"I'd still like to know where they're taking Maggie's horse," said Vince, a little exasperated. He hated not knowing what was happening.

"I'd like to know that myself!" whispered Peter Franklin, who had decided to stick close to them.

"No way am I going to – Hey, what's going on over there?" Lillian asked, pointing to the entrance to the riding stable. "Isn't that Maggie's mother? Of course! Oh no, that means that her nasty father can't be far away!"

Vince straightened his shoulders. "If that mean-spirited bully ever comes near me again, he'll be sorry!" Determined, he headed straight for Vera Bratton, who was screaming shrilly at a rider wearing show clothes. The young rider was baffled by the woman's hysterical outburst and he was visibly relieved when Vince and Lillian delivered him from Mrs. Bratton's fury, the source of which he couldn't even comprehend. "That lady isn't playing with a full deck," the rider whispered to them as he hurried away.

"Hello, Mrs. Bratt –" Vince began, but Maggie's mother interrupted him abruptly.

"He did it! He had Giaccomo taken away! I was just in the stable, and the horse is gone! Can you imagine? He really is gone! Maggie will never be able to survive the fact that her father – How can someone like that even be a father?" The woman broke down in tears.

Hesitantly Lillian went over to her and wrapped her arms around her, while Vince tried desperately to talk with her, but Mrs. Bratton seemed to be in shock. She was crying so hard that she seemed unable to take in what Vince was telling her. Even when he shouted at her, she didn't react.

"May I?" asked Peter Franklin calmly as he pushed Vince out of the way. "Please forgive me, ma'am, but there's no other way," he said, and, with a pained expression, he grabbed Mrs. Bratton by the shoulders and slapped her – hard.

Shocked, Maggie's mother took a deep breath and stared at the reporter.

"I'm truly sorry, but you sounded hysterical!" He smiled apologetically at the woman. "Are you okay? Can you listen now?"

Vera Bratton nodded weakly. She was still crying, but on the other hand she seemed more herself.

"Please, excuse me. I know I've been behaving badly, but I ... Giaccomo –" she stammered.

"Giaccomo is alive and he's fine," Vince hastened to tell her.

"What?"

Lillian nodded encouragingly. "It's true, Mrs. Bratton."

"But how is that possible? I mean, his stall ... why ... ?" Vera was incapable of speaking in complete sentences, and before Vince could explain in detail, they heard a piercing scream coming from the stable.

"What's wrong now?" The riding instructor turned around and was just about to open the door to the stable, when it opened abruptly from the inside.

Her face the color of chalk, Marina Carter, one of Vince's riding students, stumbled out of the building.

"What happened to you?" Astonished, Vince stared at the young woman, who was dressed in her riding habit.

"He's gone! My horse, Sandman, is gone! Disappeared! The stall I put him in during the breaks is empty! Vince, it's empty!" she stammered tonelessly.

Vince and Lillian turned pale and stared at each other.

"This just can't be happening," murmured Lillian and swallowed hard.

"Marina, which stall did you put Sandman in?" asked Vince, although he already knew the answer.

"The second one from the back, on the right-hand side! And I'm positive that I locked the door before I left the stable. Oh, no, where can he be?"

Sensing the young woman's desperation and confusion, Vince put his arms around her and held her gently but firmly. "Marina, I think we know where Sandman is," he told her in a reassuring voice.

The young woman's eyes widened. "Really, Vince? I'm so glad, but why are you staring at me so strangely? Is something wrong? Is there something wrong with Sandman? Come on, please tell me!"

Vince couldn't tell her right away. He simply didn't know how.

Peter Franklin looked from one to the other. He was beginning to see how the threads of this story were connected. He whistled softly.

"Now I get it! Someone had the wrong horse picked up, didn't he?" he burst out. But Marina just stared at him with watery, uncomprehending eyes.

"Picked up? What do you mean by 'picked up?'" she asked.

Vince and the reporter exchanged glances quickly.

"Do we have a chance?" the reporter asked, and Vince shrugged his shoulders.

"I have no idea. It depends."

"Could you please tell me what all of this means? What do you mean, 'Do we have a chance?' A chance for what?" Marina's voice seemed to crack. She sensed that something terrible had happened to her horse.

"Come on, let's go!" barked Vince, pulling Marina with him. "I'll explain everything to you in the car."

"I'm going with you!" called Mrs. Bratton, who in some way felt responsible for the whole mess, and she ran after them.

"And I'll stay here and be a lookout," shouted Lillian. Although she would rather have gone with them, she'd realized that neither Crissy nor Kevin knew that Giaccomo was still alive. She wanted to tell them both as soon as they got back.

"I'll follow in my own car. I have a radio and a telephone. Maybe I can reach someone who can help us find that vet's vehicle. "Did you happen to see a name or anything that could help us identify him?" Peter said to Lillian.

"I only got a brief look at the side of the van, but then Mr. Bratton told us his name was Dr. Pauley –"

"Pauley! C'mon, we'll stop that horse from being put down!" Peter Franklin was on his way to his car when he heard Marina's scream.

"Darn!" he murmured to himself angrily. "Why can't I ever keep my mouth shut?"

Marina nearly collapsed at the words "put down." It seemed like a nightmare.

"Vince! What ... oh, no!"

"Marina, pull yourself together! Don't think about it right now. If we hurry, maybe we can catch up to the van! Come on! Every minute counts!" Vince shouted to the young woman.

"My horse is being taken to be put down? Who would do such a thing? I mean –"

"Who would do that? My husband, for one. But I still can't believe it!" Vera whispered softly. "Please, Marina, come on. We've got to try to save your horse."

Devastated, Marina stared open-mouthed at Maggie's mother. She had no idea what everyone was talking about. All she knew was that her horse was missing, and these folks were offering to help her find it. So she got in Vince's SUV and sat next to Mrs. Bratton. *I have to hope that Vince and the others know what they're doing*, she thought to herself.

*

Crissy had given Evening Star his head. She didn't care where the horse took her as long as it was away from the show grounds.

Evening Star raced out of the woods and galloped along beside a narrow stream, which at some point flowed into nearby Echo Lake.

Up to now, Crissy and Maggie had always enjoyed their rides along flowing water, and they had allowed their horses to drink along the way. But today Crissy couldn't find any pleasure in riding beside the stream. On the contrary. She began to hate everything that had previously meant so much to her and Maggie, because she knew that – because of the terrible events of the day – neither one of them might ever be able to find that happiness again.

*

Kevin had almost caught up with Crissy. Sharazan had definitely gained ground on Evening Star, and it was now only a matter of time before he pulled even with Crissy.

"Crissy! Wait! Hey, why are you doing this? You won't change anything by racing around like a crazy person! Crissy, stop!" shouted Kevin loudly, but the girl paid no attention to him and just pressed her calves more tightly against Evening Star's belly.

Why can't he just leave me alone? she thought angrily. *If his girlfriend hadn't had that stupid idea of taking kids for rides, maybe we wouldn't be in this mess.*

*

Ricki, Cathy and the horses had almost arrived at their destination. They had left the woods and ridden along a bumpy path in the middle of lush, green meadows, and could now see the bright red roof of a farmhouse in the distance.

Ricki took a deep breath, her heart thumping wildly. "I hope this works," she said softly to her girlfriend, who nodded silently. "I don't know what we'll do if Carlotta turns us down," she added, but at that Cathy just shook her head.

"You don't believe that Carlotta would ever permit a healthy horse to be killed for no good reason, do you?" she said a little harshly. "First you get a great idea, and then you start to doubt it!"

Ricki was silent. She was busy rehearsing in her mind what she was going to say to the older woman. *Carlotta, you have to help us save this wonderful horse, you just have to!*

"And what are we going to do if she isn't there?" Ricki began again. They'd almost reached Mercy Ranch, the safe haven Carlotta was constructing to provide care and shelter to old, ill, abused, or unwanted horses.

"Ricki, get a grip. Where else would Carlotta be? Of course she'll be home! She has carpenters at work everywhere. You know Carlotta. Would she just turn a bunch of workmen loose with no supervision? Hey, look, there's her car over there!" Cathy pointed in the direction of the farm.

"I don't even want to imagine what Mr. Bratton is going to do when he finds out about all this!"

*

Over the constant din of the hammering, drilling, sawing, and nailing, the girls could hear the loud, unmistakable voice of Carlotta Mancini. She did not sound pleased.

"Well, sir, if I say that I want a rustic wood floor in the rooms, then I certainly don't mean parquet! What idiot delivered that stuff? Is he planning to come every day to clean up after an endless number of riding boots have walked over it? And is he willing to pay the difference in price? What? You were the idiot! Well, thanks for nothing! If you don't remove all of it immediately, you'll have to keep it clean! I'll expect you to come back tomorrow with the right kind of wood!"

Ricki and Cathy glanced at each other and slid out of their saddles.

"Sounds like Carlotta is in her element!" commented Ricki.

"Hello, you two! What are you doing here?" came the commanding voice of the former circus rider when she saw the girls from the upstairs window. "You certainly have a beautiful horse with you! Who is that? Wait a minute, I'll come down!" And leaning on the crutches that had been her support ever since the horseback-riding accident that ended her brilliant career many years before, she came limping down the main stairs, wondering what kind of adventure her young friends were involved in this time.

"Hi, Carlotta! How's it going? Making progress?" asked Cathy boldly, while Ricki, for the hundredth time, repeated her request in her mind.

"Well, if the workers had just done what I told them to, the renovation could have been finished a long time ago," grinned Carlotta and started walking toward the horses.

"My boy, I've been neglecting you lately, haven't I?" She took hold of Rashid's head lovingly, and rubbed his favorite spot behind his ears.

"Are your stalls ready yet?" asked Ricki trying ever so hard to sound only mildly interested.

Carlotta nodded. "Not all of them, but most are. I think the stable should be completely finished sometime next week, if Mr. Freeman comes in time to install the watering troughs. I'm getting too old to be hauling buckets of water several times a day to these four-legged old-timers so they can drink." She laughed her unmistakable hearty laugh and then turned to Diablo and the new horse that Ricki was holding by the reins.

"Diablo, do you have competition?"

The black horse snorted loudly and blew into her gray hair.

"This is Giaccomo," Ricki began slowly. "He belongs to a friend of ours."

Carlotta examined the brown horse with her expert's eye and pronounced him, "A beautiful animal! Your friend is lucky to be the owner of such a wonderful horse."

"Yeah, well, actually, it's not hers anymore," Ricki tried again.

"No? That's a shame! How come you brought him with you? Did one of you buy him?"

Ricki shook her head. "No, but ... well, Giaccomo ... was 'officially' put down today."

"Put down! Hmm! He looks very much alive to me," she laughed, but quickly became serious. She knew that Ricki would never joke about something like that.

"Okay, tell me all about this horse. You didn't ride over

101

here just to pass the time of day, did you? Come on, Ricki, tell me the story ... the *whole* story."

Ricki looked down at the ground. "Well, it's like this ..." she began slowly, while Carlotta listened, her gaze resting on Giaccomo.

Cathy gave an encouraging nod to her friend. She thought to herself, *Everything's going to be fine. Giaccomo won Carlotta's heart at first sight. She won't let us down.*

Chapter 7

Larry Bratton – troubled by an uneasy conscience – paced back and forth in the living room of his apartment. He'd been home for about half an hour following his unsuccessful attempt to pick up his wife at the hospital. He was puzzled. He'd expected Vera to be waiting for him, but when he showed up at the hospital, he was told she'd gone off in a taxi. No one knew where.

He was so upset by this unexpected turn of events that he decided to return home at once, without visiting his daughter. *What a coward I am*, he thought now.

He kept glancing at the wall clock, impatient for Vera's return. He couldn't imagine where she could be all this time. He needed to explain – justify – his actions to his wife. If only she would come home so that he could tell her why he – Oh, nonsense! He didn't have to explain his actions to anyone! After all, he'd gotten rid of Giaccomo for his daughter's sake, hadn't he?

Or maybe not, a voice inside him whispered. *Don't you see that by destroying your daughter's beloved Giaccomo, you've also destroyed a part of her? How can she trust you after this? How will you be able to look at her ever again?*

Larry Bratton shook his head, hoping to drive away that inner voice, but it wouldn't go away and it was making him frantic. He ran into the hallway, grabbed his car keys from the hall table, and was just about to escape from the house to clear his head when he passed Maggie's room. The door was closed. Maggie kept it that way.

He stood and stared at the doorknob for a few seconds before he began – hesitantly – to turn it. He had a low opinion of parents who intruded on their children's privacy, but he needed to learn what he could about his daughter. Maybe he didn't know her as well as he thought he did, so he stepped inside the room and looked around.

A pigsty, was his first impression, but on closer examination he began to discover a kind of order in the tangled mess of his daughter's room. Everywhere there were little things – mementos of people, places, and things – lying around or propped up on bookcases, the desktop, dresser, and other flat surfaces. They obviously meant a lot to Maggie. To many of them she'd attached handwritten notes that told when, where, why, and from whom she'd received the object.

With a mixture of respect for and curiosity about these personal items, Larry Bratton picked up a little wooden box and slowly raised the lid. Inside, on a bed of cotton, lay a lovely heart-shaped semiprecious stone that shimmered in all the colors of the rainbow when held up to the light. "For Maggie, my very best friend. I'm so glad that you are in my life. Crissy" was written on the card that was inside. He closed the lid and put the box back where he found it.

A framed photo on Maggie's desk drew his attention. It was a snapshot from last summer, when Maggie had participated in a starlight ride with Giaccomo. Beaming, the girl stood next to her tall, enormous brown horse and leaned trustingly against his muscular neck.

When he returned the photo to the desk, it toppled over, and he could see Maggie's handwriting. She had written something on the back of the photo:

You are my sun on gloomy days, my light in the darkness, a shining star on a moonless night, and the best friend that I could ever wish for! Nothing must ever separate us, because that, my wonderful Giaccomo, would destroy me. Without you, my life would be senseless!

Maggie's father sank into the desk chair, his daughter's words replaying in his head ... *my life would be senseless!* He knew that teenage girls often indulged in flights of romantic fantasy and poetic language, but this was scaring him, *Nothing must ever separate us ...*

"Oh, no," he whispered tonelessly, "what have I done? I wanted to protect my daughter, not destroy her life. She never knew how many times I almost died of fright when I saw her riding that horse."

And now you're here and you have no idea what you should do, said his inner voice.

"Yes, I do!" he shouted aloud, and he pushed himself out of the chair, ran out of his daughter's room, and headed for the kitchen. He grabbed the wall phone and dialed the number of Dr. Pauley's Animal Hospital with trembling fingers, but it just rang and rang. No one was there to answer it.

Frustrated, he left the house, jumped into his car, and sped off, tires screeching. His only chance was to drive to the animal hospital himself and tell Pauley he changed his mind – if it wasn't already too late.

*

Maggie lay in her hospital bed tossing and turning, trying to find a comfortable position. Impossible! She hurt all over.

"Well, how's our equestrienne?" the nurse asked pleasantly, as she entered Maggie's room to make up the bed. "Is everything okay? Do you want me to bring you something to read?"

Maggie shook her head. "No, thank you. I think even a magazine would be too heavy for me to hold right now."

"Is it that bad?"

Maggie didn't answer.

Nurse Rita looked at her more closely and then sat down on the edge of the bed. She stroked the girl's hand comfortingly.

"And what else?" she asked with a spontaneity that astonished Maggie.

"Why do you ask?"

"Well even a blind woman could see that something is bothering you. You can't fool me, girl!" The nurse smiled at Maggie encouragingly, but she didn't press her any further and the girl remained silent.

"I've got to go now," the nurse said after a little while. "I've got other patients to look after. If you want to talk – about anything – just ring, okay? I'll be on duty until eight o'clock tonight." Nurse Rita was almost at the door when Maggie blurted out, "I'm worried about Giaccomo."

"Who is Giaccomo? Your friend?"

"No, Giaccomo is my horse, and my father threatened to have him killed if anything happened to me while I was riding him."

"Is Giaccomo a dangerous horse?"

Maggie shook her head. "No! He's the gentlest horse in the whole world! My accident wasn't his fault. He just got spooked by a little boy who didn't know any better –" Maggie was beginning to ramble. The nurse cut her off and brought her back to the point.

"But you're scared that he might not be there when you get out of the hospital?"

"Yes," Maggie whispered quietly.

The nurse came back, sat on the edge of Maggie's bed, and embraced the sobbing girl tenderly.

"Don't worry. If God doesn't want anything to happen to your horse, then your father won't be able to do anything about it!"

Maggie held on tightly to the chubby nurse's hand and wished she never had to let her go.

"God just couldn't want Giaccomo to be put down," she stammered. "But I think, when my father decides to do something, he doesn't bother asking God for permission first!"

*

Carlotta listened closely as Ricki told her about Giaccomo and Maggie. Finally, she shook her head, outraged.

107

"It's unbelievable what some people are capable of! Of course you can leave him here for a while! There's still some straw and hay from the previous owner. But, kids, we have to think of something pretty soon, because even though Maggie's father is doing something illegal and totally wrong, what we're doing is actually against the law, too. We've taken a horse illegally and are hiding him from his rightful owner! That could have terrible consequences for us and also for the ranch." Carlotta looked at the two girls gravely.

"You're right, Carlotta. I hadn't thought it out that far ahead," Ricki admitted glumly. She certainly didn't want to get Carlotta in trouble, nor did she want to do anything that would jeopardize Mercy Ranch.

"But the rightful owner is Maggie, and not her father, isn't that true?" Cathy commented.

"Yes, it is, but since Maggie's still a minor and Mr. Bratton probably paid for the horse, he's considered the owner," explained Carlotta, glancing at Giaccomo, who was bored and scraping the ground with his hoof. All of a sudden she grinned. "Ignorance doesn't protect you from the law, but let's just assume that Maggie is in charge. Could we talk with her mother? If she would give her approval for what we're doing, we probably wouldn't get into any trouble at all."

Ricki's eyes began to shine. "Oh, Carlotta, you're the best! We'll ride right back and talk to her. I'm guessing she'll either be at the hospital with Maggie or, worst-case scenario, at home. I promise, we'll be back with written permission for what we're doing. Okay, Cathy, can we do that?"

Her friend nodded firmly. "Absolutely!"

Carlotta had taken Giaccomo's reins and Ricki was already back in the saddle.

Cathy was just about to mount, when Carlotta's voice held her back.

"No, Cathy. I think Ricki should ride back alone. You can put straw into two stalls in the stable and then see to the horses. Rashid will stay with Giaccomo. Then there won't be any problems. I'll drive you back later."

Cathy nodded. "Okay, good idea. Ricki, you'd better get going. Find Mrs. Bratton, wherever she is, but be sure Maggie's father doesn't get involved," she urged, and then she crossed her fingers for luck.

"Okay, see you later!" Ricki shouted. She turned Diablo around, and trotted away from the yard. As soon as she reached the open meadow she gave the black horse his head and, like a jockey at the Kentucky Derby, she leaned forward over his neck and whispered in his ear, "C'mon, Diablo, let's go. We've got important work to do, and every minute counts!"

*

Peter Franklin had switched on the speakerphone in his car, and while he chased after Vince's beat-up SUV, he spoke excitedly with his editor.

"Brad, I'm chasing after a horse killer," he shouted.

"Well, what do you want from me?"

"I need your help. Call the Pauley Animal Hospital and tell them they're going to be in serious trouble if they put down the horse that's on the way to them." Up ahead, Vince's car

109

had stalled, bringing it to a full stop. The reporter had to slam on his brakes to avoid rear-ending him. *Why is he stopping? There are no traffic lights around here.*

"Not only is killing the horse against the law, what's even worse – it's the wrong horse. Come on, Brad, help me out here! And then call me back, okay? Time's running out! I had no idea that Pauley's Animal Hospital was so far outside town!"

"Okay, I'll do it – talk to you later, and, Peter, make a good story out of this!"

"Yeah, yeah," grumbled Peter Franklin, hanging up.

*

In the stalled SUV in front of Peter, Vera Bratton was wringing her hands together nervously. She was trying to explain everything to Marina, but the young woman wasn't listening to her. Fear for her horse consumed her.

"Shouldn't we be there by now?" she asked Vince, fearing that the car's breakdown was going to ruin everything.

"Stay calm, Marina. I know this rusty old bucket has seen better days, but she'll get us there. We'll make it." With that, Vince restarted the engine and pushed the gas pedal to the floor. After some alarming coughing and sputtering, the old engine caught hold and they were on their way again.

*

Kevin had pushed Sharazan to the limit and finally managed to cut off Crissy, making her stop short on Evening Star.

"Are you crazy?" she yelled at the boy, who had leaned down from his saddle and grabbed her reins.

"No, but it looks like you are! Could you please tell me what good you're doing by galloping through the area like this? Do you want your horse to break a leg? That would put him in the same boat as Giaccomo!" Kevin hadn't intended to say that, and Crissy was jolted by his words. Shocked, she stared at him and the corners of her mouth began to move.

"You're right! I must have been crazy!" Upset, she looked down at Evening Star's ears, which were beginning to play back and forth.

"Can I let go of the reins now? Will you stay put?" asked Kevin, almost out of breath.

Crissy nodded. "Yes, don't worry. I'm really sorry!"

Relieved, Kevin straightened himself and sat back up in Sharazan's saddle. "Come on, Crissy, let's ride back. The others will be worried about us, and they've got enough on their minds as it is!"

"Agreed," said the girl, and she turned her horse around and joined Kevin. "Do you think we could buy Giaccomo from that nasty vet?" she asked suddenly, looking a little hopeful.

"I don't know. He's already been paid to put Giaccomo down," Kevin said slowly. "Where would we find that kind of money anyway?

"I don't know. Start thinking! We need to come up with a plan fast. There's got to be a way to save Giaccomo!" Crissy was becoming restless. "Come on, let's ride over to Dr. Pauley's hospital! It's at least worth a try!"

"And where will you get the money?" Kevin asked, as Crissy galloped off.

"I have no idea, but that isn't important now! Come on, hurry up!"

"But –" Kevin rolled his eyes. There was nothing left for him to do but gallop after her.

But it might work! he thought, as the rhythmic beat of the hooves thundered in his head.

*

Larry Bratton circled the locked-up building four times. No one was on the premises. Then he remembered that Pauley had a branch office about twenty miles away.

"Why didn't I think of that right away?" he mumbled to himself as he jumped back into his car. A glance at his watch showed him that he had wasted much too much time already. *If Giaccomo is still alive I'll go to every show that Maggie is in for the rest of my life*, he promised himself.

*

"Peter? I'm sorry, but I can't reach anybody at Pauley's by phone. You do know that today is Saturday, don't you? Dr. Pauley's hospital is closed." Brad's voice sounded a little tinny on the speakerphone in the car.

"Of course I know that it's Saturday, but if they pick up horses on Saturday, then there has to be somebody in charge on Saturday, doesn't there? Have you tried Pauley's home phone?"

"Of course, but no one picked up there either."

"Thanks anyway," he said, shutting off the speakerphone. "Time is running out for that horse!" he mumbled tensely to

112

himself, as he continued to stay close behind Vince's SUV. *I wonder what kind of a story I'll be writing?* the reporter asked himself. *Will it be about warm human caring – or cold human indifference?*

*

"We have to turn left up there," Vince said more to himself than to the other passengers, who now, for the first time during this trip, had begun exchanging tense and frightened looks.

Would they be able to save Sandman?

Vera Bratton looked out of the side window dejectedly, and suddenly her expression changed.

"That's just not possible!" she said quietly and pressed her face against the windowpane.

"Is something wrong, Vera?" Vince asked.

"Up ahead, I ... I could be wrong, but I think that's our car speeding away! Larry, my husband, must have been here!"

"And what does that mean?" asked Marina, who had the feeling that she was going to faint.

"I ... I don't know!" Helplessly, Vera shrugged her shoulders.

"Hang on, everybody. Here we go," said Vince, and he floored it.

*

Peter Franklin raised his eyebrows. "What's going on now?" he asked himself. He flashed his high beams on and off a few times and honked his horn to get Vince's attention. Finally he caught up with the riding instructor.

"Hey, what's up?" he yelled through the open window to Vince.

Vince slowed down and pointed to the disappearing car. "That's Bratton's car. Maggie's father was at Dr. Pauley's hospital," he shouted. "We're heading there now!"

The reporter nodded to show that he had understood. He looked ahead and saw the taillights of Bratton's car getting farther and farther away. "Something tells me that they're on the wrong trail," he growled to himself, and then he stepped on the gas and sped off in pursuit of Bratton.

*

"Hey, where are we going? Dr. Pauley's hospital is in the other direction!" Kevin called to Crissy.

"Yeah, but this is Saturday. Nobody works at Pauley's on Saturday. And I know where he stables his horses."

"He has a stable?"

"Sure. I think he'll have Giaccomo brought to his stable."

"Let's hope so!"

Silently, they let their animals go as fast as they dared on the narrow path.

Crissy may be right, thought Kevin. *But what if she isn't?*

*

Ricki was feeling optimistic as she trotted along the road on Diablo. It eased her mind to know that Carlotta was taking care of Giaccomo. Now, if she could just find

Maggie's mother and explain what she was doing with Giaccomo, everything would turn out well. But her momentary euphoria turned to cold panic when she saw Dr. Pauley's transporter on the other side of the street, pulled up in front of a nearby stable.

Thank goodness Giaccomo isn't inside that thing, she thought..

While Ricki gazed at the transporter, Diablo suddenly began to spook. "Calm down, boy, I promise you that you'll never have to go to that horrible vet."

She could see that the driver had gone behind the transporter and was letting down the loading ramp. Almost immediately, there was a shrill whinnying coming from inside the van. Diablo answered it right away.

"That's ... that's impossible! How did Sandman get here?" Ricki swallowed excitedly when she saw the horse emerging from the van, but then she pressed her calves against Diablo's belly.

"Come on!" she shouted. "Run, Diablo!"

As the black horse shot forward like an arrow, Ricki's thoughts raced. *Sandman shouldn't be here! He's registered for the dressage event. Marina told Crissy that she thinks she has a good chance to win with him. What does this mean?*

A man was just leading the horse to the stable as Ricki came racing toward him on Diablo.

Sandman smelled his horse friend and stopped short. He turned his head to Diablo and whinnied loudly to him.

Bewildered, the man turned around, too, and stared in amazement at the female rider who was approaching him in a full gallop, gesturing wildly.

"What's up with her?" he murmured softly.

115

"Stop!" yelled Ricki.

He stopped, looking questioningly at her.

"Please, excuse me, but that horse, how ... how did it get here?" she asked.

"You have eyes, don't you? So why do you ask?" answered Pauley, and he glanced at his watch. Not only had he had to transport this horse himself today – his employees were enjoying their day off – but now he was being confronted with dumb questions! Without paying any more attention to Ricki, he started to lead the gelding into the stable, but the girl wouldn't budge.

"Did you pick him up at the horse show? Who told you to do it? It wasn't Marina, was it?"

Pauley didn't know anyone named Marina, and when he didn't answer, Ricki urged her black horse right in front of him.

"Get out of the way! You're preventing me from doing my job!"

"Could you please answer my question? It's really important," pleaded Ricki urgently.

The man was getting furious. "Now you listen to me! I'd be very grateful if you'd get your horse away from here so that I can finish up here and go home! Come on, Jack, or whatever your name is." He jerked the rope, but Sandman remained motionless like a statue.

"Why are you calling him Jack? His name isn't Jack! It's Sandman!" After Ricki had spoken, she realized what was going on. Jack ... Giacco ... Giaccomo!

"Wait a minute!" she yelled. "Please, please, just tell me one more thing. Did Mr. Bratton give you this order? Please, you have to tell me!"

116

Pauley had managed to get Sandman around Diablo. "Yes, now get out of here! You're getting on my nerves!" Enraged, the man looked back over his shoulder.

"But that's not Giaccomo! That's Sandman, and he doesn't belong to Mr. Bratton! You ... you took the wrong horse!" screamed Ricki.

Pauley stopped in his tracks, startled. Slowly he turned around and stared at the girl with his eyes narrowed. "What did you say?"

Ricki pointed at Sandman. "That's not the horse you were supposed to pick up!"

He gazed at Sandman angrily. "Are you sure?"

"Absolutely!"

"No doubt?"

"None!" Ricki was trembling with nerves. "Sandman belongs to a friend of mine, who is actually supposed to be performing in the dressage competition on him right now!" she added in a shaky voice.

"Oh, no! That can't be true!" shouted the man. "You know what I think? You're just telling me this stuff to save this Jack! I know you kids! You're so crazy about horses you can't handle it when –"

"Sure I'm crazy about horses, but I'm not a liar!" Ricki dared to interrupt Pauley in mid sentence. "If you don't believe me, then take Sandman back and let Marina identify him. She must be beside herself with worry."

The man hesitated. Maybe the girl was telling the truth – her story was plausible, but ...

"I don't have any reason to believe you! Listen, if you are telling the truth, this Marina can come and get the horse by producing her owner's papers. If not –" Pauley threw his hands up in exasperation, "If not, then this is none of your business."

Ricki trembled and turned pale. "Couldn't you call the Avalon Riding Academy? They would confirm what I'm telling you," she asked, scared.

"No," Pauley snorted furiously. "A commission is a commission! I need tangible, verifiable proof. If you want to prove to me that it's the wrong horse, then ride back and bring the real owner – with her certificate of ownership – back with you! Understand?"

Ricki nodded.

"So! What are you waiting for?" he yelled at her, and finally led Sandman into the stable. "And you'd better hurry, because tomorrow morning he'll be taken away."

"But tomorrow, tomorrow is Sunday!" Ricki was so upset that she could hardly speak.

"That's right, but this Sunday I have work to do. Now get out of here!" he shouted from the stable.

With a loud sob, Ricki wheeled Diablo around on his hind legs and galloped off.

Chapter 8

"No one's here!" Vince called from the parking lot. Vera and Marina just shrugged their shoulders helplessly. They'd gone around Dr. Pauley's hospital several times, peering in windows, trying doorknobs, but it seemed to be completely abandoned.

"Now what? What are we going to do now?" Marina was becoming panicky. "I want my horse back!" she cried to herself softly.

Vera went to her and tried to comfort her, but she was pushed brusquely aside.

"Don't touch me!" Marina screamed loudly, and when Vera saw the pain in the young woman's face she knew that it was Larry's action that put it there, and that even though she'd had nothing to do with Sandman's disappearance, Marina held her responsible for it. Vera felt very guilty – and angry at Larry. His stubborn foolishness had brought sorrow to two innocent young women, and one of them was his daughter.

"Calm down, Marina," Vince tried to comfort her, but the young woman just stared at him with hard, hate-filled eyes. She turned suddenly and ran off.

"Marina, stay here! Where are you going? Don't do anything crazy, now!" Vince reached out to grab her arm, but Marina twisted away from him and disappeared behind the building.

Vera turned pale. "Come on, Vince, we've got to find her." They ran after her, but Marina was nowhere to be seen and she didn't respond to their calls.

"She can't just have disappeared into thin air!" panted Vera.

"No, of course not." Perplexed, Vince looked around, but it was clear that Marina didn't want to be found.

"We can't leave her here alone," exclaimed Vera, who was comparing her to her daughter. Maggie would have done the same thing. First she would have disappeared, and then she would have tried to find her horse herself.

"Now, come on, Marina, don't act like a child!" Vince called out, but the young woman remained silent and out of sight.

She was crouched down in a dark corner between the transport vans. *Why don't you just leave? Go, all of you! I just want to be left alone! Why can't you understand that?* Marina pressed her hands firmly against her ears to block out the sound of Vince and Vera's calls. She was definitely not going to get into the car again with the wife of the man who was responsible for what was happening to her horse.

"I think she's old enough to know what she's doing," said Vince quietly, and he motioned to Vera to get into the car.

"But ... but she's very upset just now. Who knows what the child will do?" Vera's maternal instincts were taking over, but Vince just waved her concerns aside.

"Come on, Mrs. Bratton, we have to try to reach Pauley at home."

"Do you know his home address?" Vera asked hopefully.

"No," Vince admitted, "but there must be a way to find it."

"Why didn't we do that right at the beginning?"

"Because, in our hysteria, we've all become idiots! I left my cell phone back at the riding academy, so we'll have to drive to a telephone booth. I should be able to get his phone number and address from Information."

Vince got into the SUV, but Vera hung back. "I think I should stay here. I don't feel right about leaving Marina alone just now," she said quietly.

Vince nodded hesitantly. "Well, okay! I'll come back here and pick you up, as soon as I find Pauley's address. Keep looking for Marina, and see if you can calm her down some."

*

Ricki and Diablo galloped at full speed along the strip of meadow that ran beside the country road. All the while, Ricki was sending up a steady stream of prayers and pleas that she would find Marina at the show. She dismissed the idea of spending time trying to locate Maggie's mother. After all, Giaccomo was no longer at immediate risk, but poor Sandman was now at the center of this mess, although he was completely unconnected to the events that brought it about.

What am I going to do if I can't find her on the show grounds? Ricki couldn't bear to think about it.

Kevin and Crissy were coming toward Ricki on their horses. *What's she doing here?* the boy asked himself, bewildered, when he saw Ricki and Diablo galloping in their direction.

Ricki was jolted out of her musings when Diablo whinnied a happy greeting to Sharazan and Evening Star. She pulled on the reins so tightly that he came sliding to a halt in front of the other horses.

"Are you crazy? Don't you know it's dangerous to gallop that fast along the side of the road?" Kevin looked concerned, but Ricki just shook her head and tried to catch her breath.

"Boy, am I glad to see you two! Pauley has –" she began, but Crissy just motioned her to stop.

"That's what we thought. Giaccomo is in Pauley's stable, isn't he? We were just on our way to him to ask him, if –"

"You've got it all wrong!" Ricki sat up a little straighter in the saddle. "Giaccomo is fine! He's at Carlotta's ranch!"

"What?" Crissy's heart jumped for joy. "Where?"

"At Mercy Ranch?" Kevin was astonished. "How did he get there? I thought, I mean, well –"

"No time to explain!" exploded Ricki. "Cathy and I took him to Carlotta for safe-keeping so that Bratton can't locate him when he finds out that he had the wrong horse picked up."

Crissy and Kevin exchanged puzzled glances.

"What do you mean, 'wrong horse?'" Kevin asked.

"Pauley mistakenly picked up Marina's Sandman instead of Giaccomo, and he intends to have him put down tomorrow, unless Marina shows up at his office with her ownership papers, proving that Sandman belongs to her and not to Bratton. Understand? We have to ride back to the show grounds right away and find Marina before it's too late!" Ricki gave her two friends some time to digest what she had told them.

"Poor Marina," whispered Crissy, as white as a sheet.

"I'd say it's more like poor Sandman," replied Kevin. "Hey, watch out! Here comes a lunatic!" shouted Kevin suddenly and pointed to the road, where a car going dangerously fast was approaching.

"Get over on the side!" yelled Ricki, and she urged Diablo farther back onto the meadow. "Come on, get going!" she called again, but Kevin and Crissy were already behind her on their horses.

"I bet it's some kids drag racing," said Kevin, as a second speeding car came into view.

"They should be arrested!" commented Crissy, a look of disgust on her face "Hey, that's Mr. Bratton!" she called out.

"Are you sure?" Kevin asked.

"Of course! I know that car! I've ridden in it often enough!" Crissy became very upset.

I wonder where he's going in such a hurry? Ricki asked herself and shortened Diablo's reins a little, to be on the safe side. She was afraid the sound of the car engines would spook him.

*

"Hey, Bratton, slow down! Don't you see the horses up

123

ahead?" murmured Peter Franklin, who slowed down immediately when he saw the group of riders on horseback in the meadow beside the road. He had just glanced briefly at the young people, but after he had gone about a hundred yards farther, he stepped on the brakes and looked into the rearview mirror.

Wasn't that the girl who had ridden away with Giaccomo? Of course! It had to be! He made a U-turn in the middle of the road, and drove back to the group in the meadow.

"Stop!" the reporter called from his car window to the three riders.

"Who's that?" asked Crissy, and Kevin just shrugged his shoulders as an answer.

"Hey, Mr. Franklin! What are you doing here?" Ricki called to him.

"I'm looking for –"

"Sandman?" burst out Ricki.

Peter Franklin nodded, bewildered. "How do you know that?"

Ricki just waved her hand dismissively. "Coincidence! Really, it's a total coincidence!"

Then she told him where and how she had discovered the horse.

"And now we have to find Marina, because –"

When Ricki had finished her story, Peter Franklin shook his head firmly. "Marina drove to Dr. Pauley's hospital with the riding instructor and Mrs. Bratton to look for the horse!"

"Oh, no! And if they didn't find him they could be anywhere, couldn't they?" Ricki's hands began to shake again.

"If we don't get Marina to come here, Sandman is lost! What should we do now? Mr. Franklin, don't you have any ideas?"

After what seemed like an eternity to the friends, he cleared his throat. "Well, I'd suggest the following. One of you should ride back to the show grounds to see if Marina is there. Another one should ride toward Pauley's place, since it is possible that she's still there. I saw her there just a few minutes ago. Ricki should ride back to Pauley's stable, and I'll drive there, too. Let's see if we can get that butcher to give us the horse somehow!"

"Well, I hope you're right, Mr. Franklin!" responded Ricki, who was uncomfortable about meeting up with the unpleasant Pauley again.

"Good, then let's do it! Crissy, can you ride back to the show?" asked Kevin, and the girl nodded, relieved. She was glad that she didn't have to go anywhere near Dr. Pauley.

"Everything all set? Okay, let's go!" ordered Peter Franklin, and he waited until the three riders had ridden off.

"So, Pauley, now let's do a little research!" he murmured quietly and switched on his car phone again.

"Who dares to disturb me on my day off?" a surly voice rasped on the other end of the line.

"Hello, Mike, this is Peter."

"Not again!"

The reporter had to grin. He was picturing his friend and colleague, Mike Sutter, sitting in a lounge chair on his patio in his bathrobe. Mike probably had a pot of coffee in front of him, as he usually did on Saturdays, and was in the process of reading through several sports columns to bring himself up to date. Mike was the least athletic man Peter knew. His favorite sport was sitting in the sun and eating junk food.

"You've been lounging around long enough, pal. I need your help!" laughed Franklin into the telephone. "You remember the story about the illegal horse trading last year?"

Mike Sutter, who had been all ready to tell Peter to get lost, sat up abruptly from his comfortable seat.

"Of course! Valuable horses kept disappearing, and they were sold with faked papers. There was a local vet from around here who was involved in it, wasn't there? Unfortunately, they couldn't prove their case against him, but let me tell you, Peter, one of these days I'm going to get that guy. Now I remember – his name was Pauley. I hear that scam is still going on."

"How'd you like to make some trouble for that guy? I mean, we could make a few allegations, let him take some heat –"

"Definitely!" Mike Sutter roared. "What's he up to now? This time he won't get away with it!"

"I'll tell you shortly. Listen, get dressed and I'll be at your place in five minutes!"

"Okay!"

Mike threw down the telephone and rubbed his hands in anticipation. If everything went well, he would finally have the proof needed to expose some of the organization's ringleaders. That would certainly be worth a raise in his boss's eyes. Peter was a real friend, even though he worked for the competition.

Vince, Maggie's mother, and Marina hadn't returned to the show grounds yet, and when Crissy arrived the only person she saw was Lillian.

"Terrific! You guys left me here alone! Where's Kevin? And where were you?" Lillian burst out, annoyed.

Crissy jumped down elegantly from Evening Star's saddle.

"By the way, Giacco is –" began Lillian.

"I already know! And I know about the situation with Sandman."

Lillian was astonished. "How?"

"We ran into Ricki. Sandman is in Pauley's stable, outside of town. Where's Marina? She has to go there if she wants to get her horse back alive!"

"I have no idea. She's probably still looking for Sandman with Vince. Anyway, she's not here," answered Lillian, sadly.

"Then let's hope Kevin has better luck. He rode over to Dr. Pauley's place, because –"

"What about Ricki? You saw her?" interrupted Lillian. "Where is she? Come on, tell me!"

Crissy rolled her eyes. "If you let me finish, you'll find out! Well, she rode back to Pauley's stable and that reporter ... " Crissy told her everything briefly, and when she had finished, she and Lillian took Evening Star to his stall and made sure he had whatever he needed.

"I could really use a soda," groaned Crissy, who was covered in dust and sweat from her ride.

"Not a bad idea," Lillian nodded in agreement. "Let's go

sit where we can see the entrance to the parking lot, so we don't miss Vince when he gets back."

*

About halfway to Pauley's other site, Larry Bratton let his car roll to a stop along the side of the road. He didn't know why, but he just couldn't keep going.

This is ridiculous, he thought. *Why would he take the horse to the other facility? No, it's too far away!* He pictured in his mind the photo of the smiling Maggie with Giaccomo, evidence of a happiness he was about to destroy.

He was amazed to discover that he was crying. He couldn't even remember the last time he had done that.

When he had himself under control again, he grabbed his cell phone and dialed his own home number, but Vera didn't seem to be home yet. He wondered if she had returned to the hospital to be with Maggie.

Larry blew his nose loudly. With determination he dialed Vera's cell phone number and hoped that wherever she was she had her cell phone switched on.

*

Beep ... beep. Vera jumped as the cell phone in her jacket pocket began to ring. She had completely forgotten she had it with her!

She could have saved Vince time searching for a phone booth. *He's right – Our panic has turned us into idiots!*

"Yes?" she answered quickly, and began to tremble as she recognized her husband's voice.

128

"Vera, I —" began Larry awkwardly, but his wife wasn't going to make it easy for him. With her eyes closed, silently she listened to his feeble apology before she answered him. "So you're sorry! You should be! Pauley picked up the wrong horse!" she said brusquely.

Larry groaned loudly. "No! But where is Giaccomo?" he asked almost inaudibly.

"Honestly, I have no idea where your daughter's horse is!" answered Vera truthfully. She had absolutely no inkling where Mercy Ranch was located. "It would be good if you came to Dr. Pauley's hospital. I'm trying to find the young woman whose horse they took. She's run away and is hiding here because she's scared to death for her horse!"

"I'll be right there," whispered Larry tonelessly into the phone, and let it drop onto the passenger seat before he drove off. He had the feeling that this was going to be the most difficult journey of his life.

He couldn't allow himself be happy about the fact that Giaccomo had been saved, so to speak, because he now knew that he had drawn a completely innocent person into this mess, through his uncontrollable rage.

"Oh, no, oh, no," he murmured over and over. "What I've done is unforgivable!"

*

Peter Franklin had driven about a mile when his car began to stall and wheeze to a stop.

"Not again!" the reporter mumbled and knocked on the gas gauge with his knuckles. It plummeted from Full to Empty.

129

"Darn car!" he cursed, and got out in order to get the gas can out of the trunk. As he picked it up, however, he was shocked by how light it was.

"Empty!" Frustrated, he threw the can back in the trunk and kicked a tire. Then he got back behind the steering wheel and grabbed his car phone to reach Mike Sutter. Mike's phone, however, rang unheard in the living room, because he was already standing outside, waiting for his friend to pick him up.

*

In the meantime, Ricki was already very near the stable where Sandman had been brought. Pauley's transporter was no longer visible, but there was an old pickup truck parked there now.

Ricki had a bad feeling when she saw the truck. Cautiously, she led Diablo nearer to the stable in the shadow of the trees and bent down in the saddle, as a second car drove up onto the gravel driveway and two men got out.

At first she thought that one of the men was the reporter, but Peter Franklin was nowhere to be seen.

Where is he? thought Ricki, and sensed that Diablo was getting nervous.

"Stand still, boy," she whispered to her horse quietly and slid out of the saddle. "Do you think I can leave you here for a while? I don't know why, but I have the feeling that those two are up to no good." Ricki undid a part of his bit so that she could tie the black horse onto one of the trees with the reins.

"I'll be right back," she comforted him, and stroked his

neck once more. Then she ran over to the stable cautiously, where the two men had disappeared.

Unnoticed, she felt her way along the wall of the building, and every once in a while she peered into a window.

Suddenly, she heard voices and immediately stood still, listening intently.

"Pauley called me. Told me to look over the brown horse and see if I'm interested in him." A bleating laugh gave Ricki goose bumps. "That idiot actually picked up the wrong horse, but it looks like it's a great horse that could be worth a few dollars."

"What?! That's risky! The owner could turn up here and –"

"By the time he comes, we'll be long gone! Pauley said there was a girl who recognized the horse when he brought him here."

"Oh, terrific! It gets better and better! No thanks, I had enough drama last time!"

"Man, Cody, don't be such a coward! Pauley sent the little brat back to Avalon to tell the owner. You know, she can get her horse back, but she needs to show proof of ownership! By the time she gets here it'll be at least an hour, and by then we'll be out of here! Anyway, Pauley has a plan! You've seen that rundown mare back at the veterinary hospital, haven't you?"

"Yeah, so?" asked Cody.

"I want you to drive over there right away and get that beast! Then we'll put it in the stall in place of the gelding, so when the owner arrives Pauley can claim that the brat must have been mistaken, since the only horse here will be the mare!"

"Genius! And what are you going to do while I'm gone?"

"Me? I'm going to drive over to Mirko's. The gelding has to be shipped out of state today!"

"Okay, I'll be back in about fifteen minutes."

"Good. Then get going. Pauley should be back any time now."

Quickly, they walked away down the aisle of the stable.

Ricki crouched behind a bush and pressed herself against the wall.

I hope they don't see Diablo, she worried, and pleaded silently with her horse not to whinny, but she needn't have bothered. Diablo behaved perfectly.

When Ricki heard the sound of the cars' engines getting farther and farther away, she stood up and peered around the corner. Everything around her was suddenly dead silent.

In her mind, she replayed fragments of the conversation she had just overheard, and she realized that she had to act immediately if Marina was ever to see Sandman again.

She looked down the road, hopeful, but she still couldn't see Peter Franklin's car.

For a moment, Ricki was at a loss as to what she should do, but then she straightened her shoulders and ran. She had to hurry if she didn't want to run into Pauley.

Quickly, she opened the unlocked stable door and ran down the aisle to where Sandman was tied up.

"Hey, you! Are you okay?" she asked the horse and, with trembling fingers, tried to untie the knot in the reins that tethered him to the stall. She finally succeeded. Nervously, she grabbed Sandman's halter and pulled him forward firmly.

"Come on! Come on, come on! If Pauley sees us, we'll be goners!"

Ricki knew that she was racing against time, and that each step Sandman took away from the stable was a step toward freedom … and life.

Finally, they left the building. The girl shut the door with her foot and then let Sandman trot.

They soon reached Diablo, who was waiting obediently for his owner. He snorted softly to greet her and his horse friend.

"Quiet!" Ricki whispered nervously. "Please, be quiet!"

She buckled Diablo's snaffle with still-shaky hands and then lifted herself into the saddle.

"Come on, you two! Let's go! Sandman, run, run for your life!" she commanded. When she could see that Sandman was trying to stay right next to Diablo, she even dared to gallop, and soon Ricki was in the woods with the two animals, far away from the road and out of sight. And not a minute too soon. Just then, Pauley turned into the stable's driveway.

Chapter 9

When Vince returned to Dr. Pauley's hospital, he spotted Larry Bratton wandering aimlessly about the grounds, his shoulders slumped in dejection. He was walking away from Vera, who was holding a sobbing Marina in her arms. *I wonder how Vera managed to coax the kid out of her hiding place*, Vince asked himself.

As Vince got out of his SUV, he glared at Maggie's father with disgust and muttered, "Horse murderer!" Then he put his arms around Marina's shoulders and led her to his car.

"I tracked down the phone number and address of Pauley's home and other facility, and I called, but no one's picking up at either place!" he explained to Vera as they walked to the SUV.

"What should we do now?" she asked, her voice trembling.

Vince just shrugged his shoulders. Gently, he helped Marina into the back seat, and Vera sat down beside her, avoiding eye contact with her husband.

"I think we should drive back to the riding academy first," replied Vince, and got in himself. Without paying any attention to Larry Bratton, he started the engine and drove off.

Maggie's father walked mechanically to his car. The fact that Vera had gone in the other vehicle had hurt him, because it showed him how little respect she had for him. *I'd have preferred it if she'd screamed at me,* he thought ruefully.

Exhausted and emotionally drained, he followed Vince's SUV slowly. He stared straight ahead, and as a result didn't notice the young man in the rearview mirror waving wildly at him. Kevin had arrived at Dr. Pauley's hospital only a few seconds before and watched the car driving away.

"Sharazan, we were too slow!" he said to his horse. He paused briefly and then turned his horse around. Avalon Riding Academy was pretty far away, and anyway, he was too concerned about his girlfriend, who was probably in Pauley's stable right now. Well, at least Peter Franklin was there, too. Nevertheless, Kevin decided to ride to Pauley's so that he could accompany Ricki back to the riding academy.

*

Ricki had ridden through the woods with no specific destination in mind. She just wanted to get as far away as possible from Pauley's stable, and to do it as quickly as possible. She was sure that the man would follow her once he discovered that she had freed Sandman. Then she saw the roof of the main building of Mercy Ranch ahead of her.

"Carlotta, of course!" She could take Sandman there. Why hadn't she thought of that before?

135

She allowed the horses to gallop again and raced the last few yards across the open field toward the ranch.

Cathy, who was just sweeping up a bit of straw in front of the stable, jumped aside, startled, as Ricki used all of her strength to halt the two animals.

"Where did you come from? And why do you have Sandman with you? Did you find Maggie's mother?" Questions were bursting out of Cathy, but Ricki just threw her the end of Sandman's lead rope.

"Take him into the stable, quick!" she yelled at her friend.

"But –"

"Right now! I'll explain everything later! We can't let that horse be seen by anyone!"

Quickly, Cathy led Sandman past the bewildered Carlotta, who had come outside to see who was shouting in her front yard.

"Ricki? What's going on?" she asked, shaking her head. "Whose horse is that? It's not another one destined for Dr. Pauley's hospital, is it?"

Ricki blushed. "Yes, it is! Please, Carlotta, I need your help again!" she said as she led Diablo into the stable. She was afraid that Pauley would turn up and recognize her and her horse.

"I'll explain everything!" shouted Ricki to Carlotta, who stood leaning on one crutch.

"Well, I have to say, I'm really curious," Carlotta answered as she limped after the two girls.

*

Kevin had decided to ride along the main road, when he suddenly thought he was seeing a mirage. Peter Franklin was running toward the town with his gas canister under his arm.

"Um… Aren't you going in the wrong direction?" asked the boy innocently, and received an answer that sounded something like a wolf growl.

"What happened to Ricki? And Sandman?"

"I have no idea!" Peter Franklin swung his empty canister. "I hope she was smart enough to ride back to the riding academy when she saw that I wasn't coming! And you should do the same thing!"

Kevin hesitated, but then he realized that the reporter's suggestion was a good one. If Ricki really was on her way back to Avalon, then Sharazan would make the trip to Pauley's stable for nothing.

"I guess you're right. But what's going to happen to Sandman?" he asked.

"As soon as I get some gas, I'll drive straight to Pauley's! I promise!"

Kevin nodded, relieved. Then he grinned broadly and pointed at his saddle. "I have some space up here. Can I give you a lift?"

Peter Franklin looked doubtful. "I'm not sure –"

At that moment, they heard a horn honking down the road. It was Mike Sutter, who'd gotten tired of waiting for his friend and was out looking for him. He pulled up beside them and stuck his head out the window.

"What's up, Peter? Thinking of taking riding lessons?"

"Am I glad to see you, Mike. And glad that you figured out that I messed up again. I ran out of gas, and Kevin here was going to offer me a lift –"

"No need to stress that animal, Peter. Get in." The two reporters waved good-bye to Kevin and took off.

Mike's car practically flew down the road, and the two men soon reached Pauley's stable, which seemed to be deserted.

"Now, I'm really curious," said Peter Franklin. He and Mike could hardly wait to expose Pauley as a crook but, unfortunately, today didn't seem to be their day. They entered the stable but, other than a small white bony mare, there was no other horse there.

"Where's the brown horse?" Peter Franklin wondered aloud.

"What brown horse?" replied a gruff voice. It was Pauley, who had followed them into the stable. He stood glaring at the two men with an icy grin on his face.

"Don't play games with us, you creep! You know exactly which horse we mean!" said Mike sharply.

"A brown horse? Hmm, yeah, now I remember." The vet pretended to think it over. "I was supposed to pick up an injured brown horse from the riding stable, but, sorry, there was no brown horse there. Instead, I picked up this white mare. You're welcome to the owner's address, if you don't believe me," he grinned ominously. "The horse is here to be treated for a leg ailment."

"You might as well admit that Sandman was in this stall! After all, the girl saw him!" Peter Franklin advised him.

"You'll have to prove that!" he challenged. "And, as far as that girl goes, she seemed very mixed up to me. How else do you suppose she got a white horse confused with a brown one? Huh?"

Mike made a fist. "I'll tell you one thing, Pauley, I know

138

that you're lying to us, and I promise you, we'll prove it! So don't be too sure of yourself!"

Pauley picked up a pitchfork and pointed it threateningly in their direction. "It's been swell talking with you gentlemen, and now I'd like to ask you to get off of my property, before things get ugly!"

"We'll be back!" Peter responded softly, and motioned to his friend. "Come on, Mike! Let's go!"

"Darn it! He made fools of us again!" cried Mike, after they had gotten back into his car. "I can feel it in my bones! And all because you didn't get enough gas for that old lemon of yours!"

Peter shrugged his shoulders. "Hmm ... It's going to be difficult to catch him at it. I think we should get together again in the next few days and figure out an airtight plan to expose him and the whole illegal horse-selling operation. If we crack it, I'll bet there'll be raises for both of us. But right now, the only thing that interests me is where Sandman and Ricki are!"

"Then let's drive back to the riding academy. If we find the riding instructor who you told me about, maybe he can tell us more."

"Good, but first I have to get to a gas station. By the way, I could go for a pizza. Want to join me when we're through at Avalon?" Peter asked his friend.

"Sure! You may be buying me lots of dinners in the future anyway, because it'll be your fault if we don't crack this story and I don't get that raise."

"Well, if that's the way it is, I guess the drinks will be on me, too!" Peter smiled at his friend, who clapped him on the shoulder.

"That's more like it!" he said, and the two men drove off together.

*

As soon as Peter and Mike left, Pauley grabbed his cell phone.

"Mirko, you can forget about the whole thing. Someone stole the nag right out of my stable!" he said angrily, and then switched off the phone when he heard a loud, jeering laugh coming from the other end of the line.

Grinding his teeth, Pauley left the stable. "But there'll be other horses!" He was sure of it.

*

Vince was sitting in the members' lounge of the academy's riding club with Vera and Marina, while Larry, whom no one had invited to join them, stood at the door feeling like a leper.

"We have to decide what to do next," the riding instructor was saying as the phone rang.

Vera wanted to get up to answer it, but Vince motioned her to let it go.

"Let it ring! Sandman is more important right now!" he said, but when it wouldn't stop ringing he picked up the receiver, somewhat annoyed.

"Avalon Riding Academy. Ricki? What's going on? ... What? ... Say that again. Yeah ... okay, we'll be right there. What? Of course ... all right. Ricki, I could kiss you! 'Bye." Vince laughed delightedly and placed the old-fashioned receiver back on the hook.

140

Everyone in the room stared at him, waiting to hear what had happened. His eyes rested on Marina's face.

"Marina, Sandman is alive! And he's fine! Ricki found him and we're supposed to – Marina? Uh-oh!" Vince just managed to spring forward in time to catch Marina, who had fainted at the mention of her horse's name. He placed her gently on the leather couch.

Just then Lillian and Crissy came rushing through the door. "Why didn't you tell us that you'd gotten back? We've been standing downstairs in the hot sun forever!" shouted Lillian, good-naturedly.

"Sandman is alive!" Crissy burst out, feeling great. "Ricki found him and Marina is supposed to go to Pauley's stable right – Is something wrong? You all look so weird." Then she caught her breath when she saw Marina lying on the couch.

"Good grief! What's wrong with her?" Lillian asked with concern.

Vince grinned. "The news that her horse is all right literally knocked her out!" he said, "She'll be fine." Both Crissy and Lillian breathed sighs of relief.

"Well, if that's all it is, then everything's okay!"

Marina opened her eyes. "I didn't just dream all of this, did I?" she asked softly, but when she saw the smiling face of the riding instructor, she knew that Sandman was safe. She was so happy she even forgave Larry Bratton right on the spot. He stood at the door with tears in his eyes, and could hardly believe what he'd just heard.

Slowly, Marina got up and, with Vince's help, walked over to him. After a little hesitation, she smiled weakly and stretched out her hand to him.

"Will you promise me something?" she asked softly, and Larry reached for her hand.

"Whatever you want," he answered hoarsely.

"We won't ever tell your daughter about all this! Okay? Never! But in exchange, you have to try to see Giaccomo for what he really is – a member of your family. Don't ever attempt to destroy your daughter's happiness again! I'm telling you this from my own personal experience. It would be the worst thing you could ever do!"

Larry nodded, and looked down at the floor. "I think I understand now," he said quietly, and Vera knew that he was serious.

Vince cleared his throat. "Well, if that's the case, then all I did today was sit in the judges' stand. I heard and saw nothing!" he laughed.

Crissy and Lillian exchanged glances.

"Okay! But considering the fact that we spent the entire day taking kids on rides, we didn't collect nearly enough money for the poor parentless children!" commented Crissy, winking.

"That's true!" added Lillian. "A certain large donation for the orphanage is still missing," she said with emphasis. Even Larry Bratton had to laugh at that.

"Okay, I get it!" he said. "You'll get your donation, won't they, Vera?"

His wife just smiled at him. "That's a promise. Now, let's get going so Marina can hug her horse again. We keep talking and talking, but the poor girl wants to get out of here!"

Everyone agreed, and soon after Maggie's parents, Sandman's owner, and Lillian, who was the only one who knew how to get to Mercy Ranch, were on their way in the

Brattons' car. Lillian noticed that Marina and Larry were both beaming.

*

"It took some doing to convince Peter Franklin that he shouldn't write an article for the paper about what happened yesterday," explained Ricki the next morning to her friend Cathy. "But at last he agreed to wait until he has proof of Dr. Pauley still being involved in illegal horse sales and then bust that story instead. One way or another, I don't think Dr. Pauley will be running his animal hospital for much longer."

"I hope not! And I'm glad something like that doesn't happen every day! Poor Marina! I'm so happy that everything ended well for Sandman."

Lillian peered from behind Holli's croup. "Well, I don't think I'd have reacted as well as Marina did in that situation. I wouldn't have cared one way or the other if the newspaper had printed something about Larry Bratton! Plus, I don't think I would have been able to forgive him so quickly for what he did to Sandman! How about you two?"

Ricki shrugged her shoulders. "I have no idea. I hope I never get into a situation like that so that I have to think about it. But you're right. Marina is really cool. Totally nice!"

"And smart!" grinned Kevin, who was leaning against the wall with his arms folded in front of him.

"What do you mean?"

"You mean you didn't hear?"

"Hear what?"

"Tell us!"

"Yeah, stop torturing us!"

Kevin laughed. "No! I'm not going to tell you anything! We're going to the show grounds today, aren't we?" he changed the subject quickly.

"Weren't we going to visit Maggie today?" Lillian asked

"That's right!" Ricki nodded. "What do you think? Should we go to the hospital first, or after the show tonight?"

"After!" responded Cathy spontaneously. "Then, at least we'll have something to tell her."

"You can say that again," replied Kevin without thinking.

"I'm not even going to ask you why."

"Good! Shall we go?"

"Yeah!"

The friends left the Sulais' stable, each one in a great mood, and sprang onto their bikes to ride to Avalon. Today there would be three levels of jumping competitions.

"If we hurry, maybe we'll get there in time to see Samantha Nolan perform again. That woman is really awesome!" Lillian's eyes began to shine as she spoke about her dressage idol.

"Then what are we waiting for?" yelled Cathy and she began to pedal furiously.

*

"Well, you can think what you like, but I think the atmosphere at a horse show is something special. Too bad I'll never participate in an event, especially jumping," said Ricki, with a glance at the obstacles that were being set up for the advanced level.

144

"Why wouldn't you? Diablo would be a perfect horse for dressage," commented Cathy, but Ricki just waved her comment aside.

"Not because of Diablo," the girl laughed. "I'd probably embarrass him. Hey, here come Marina and Crissy."

"Hi! It's great that you guys are here so early. You're going to keep your fingers crossed for Marina, aren't you?" asked Crissy, happily.

"Why should we? There isn't another dressage event today, is there?" Lillian asked.

"No. Dressage is over," laughed Marina and pointed over to the jumping area. "I thought I'd try my hand at jumping again."

"I didn't know Sandman's a jumper."

"He is, but he's not very good at it. Not good enough for the advanced level, anyway. Actually, a rider had to cancel, and I'm going to take her place," explained Marina, and pulled the jumping event identification bracelet a little tighter around her wrist.

"Oh! That sounds great. Then you're going to ride her horse?"

Marina nodded. "Yeah, that is, if it gets here in time. If it doesn't arrive soon, then it's going to be very tight. I'd better go look," Marina turned to go.

"What number are you?" called Cathy after her.

"Thirteen." came the reply. "I'll see you after the jumping event, okay?"

"Okay! Good luck!"

"Thanks!" Marina and Crissy disappeared among a crowd of spectators all jostling for the best seats for the event.

"Do any of you know which horse she's riding?" asked Ricki.

"I have no idea, but isn't thirteen an unlucky number?"

"Oh, Cathy, just cut it out! Since when are you superstitious?" Lillian protested.

"Hey, I think they're finished setting up the obstacles." Kevin glanced at his watch. "It's supposed to begin in about forty-five minutes. I think I'll just have time to get something to eat first. I saw the refreshment stand back there."

"Kevin, if you didn't eat all the time, you'd be half the man you are today," quipped his girlfriend.

"You'd better believe it. Do you all want some breakfast, too, or do you want to wait here? We could go over to the area where they walk the horses after the jump. And didn't you want to see Samantha Nolan?"

"Oh, I completely forgot about her! And her performance is so early. Are you guys coming with me?" Lillian didn't even wait for her friends' answer, but just took off. How could she have been so lame brained as to forget the main reason she'd even come back today?

*

Things were already bustling. The first horses were being saddled and warmed up, and riders were discussing the obstacles. Here and there, excited chatter could be heard as the show arena slowly filled with spectators.

Ricki closed her eyes and listened to the snappy show music being played over loudspeakers. *Thirty more minutes*, she thought. On one hand, she was glad to be only an observer at this event, although she had often dreamed about flying over the obstacles on her wonderful black horse. However, she was honest enough to admit to herself that she would probably be the only one flying – right out of the saddle!

Ricki was torn from her daydream by an announcement on the loudspeaker. The course had been opened for the participants' inspection. Ricki watched Marina as she walked around the obstacle course.

"It looks like it's about to start," said Kevin a little while later, as he sat next to her in the stands, finishing the last of his egg salad sandwich.

"Well then, let's keep our fingers crossed for Marina. Hey, Kevin, now that I see the obstacles I wonder … do you think Maggie would have had a chance to win on Giaccomo?" Ricki asked. Excited, she watched the first rider as he skillfully guided his horse over the fences. By the end of the course he had eight faults.

"Hmm, it's hard to say," responded Kevin. "I think maybe Giaccomo might have made it, but Maggie? If you're afraid of jumping, it doesn't work. You know the old saying, 'Throw your heart over the fence and the rest will follow!' I think Maggie might have held onto her heart, instead of throwing it over the fence."

While they were chatting the second rider finished the course and rode toward the exit in a bad mood. Soon after, he led his horse past Ricki and Kevin.

"The triple combination is set up totally tight! You need more luck than skill to get through that without any faults," he commented to one of the grounds crew. "With two falls, I might as well give up!"

Ricki, who had listened to the last rider with only one ear, poked Kevin in the side. "Come on, let's go stand near the entrance, and then we can tell Marina to be careful on the combination jumps!"

The two of them left the stands quickly and ran to get into position along the fence that separated the spectators from the arena.

One after another, the riders came through and tried their luck, but only a very few managed to ride the entire course with less than four faults.

Finally, it was Marina's turn.

As the number thirteen was called out, Ricki turned to look for Marina so that she could give her the information about the combination jumps. But as Marina rode past her, smiling, Ricki choked on the words. With astonishment, she saw Giaccomo, prancing nervously toward the entrance.

"Wish us luck," whispered Marina to Ricki. "I want to win for Giaccomo and Maggie!" Then she straightened her shoulders, rode past the judges' stand in perfect dressage position, and greeted her friends with a slight nod.

Vince, who was standing with the point judges, crossed his fingers on both hands for her. *You'll make it!* he signaled Marina, and she gave him the slightest nod.

When the starting bell rang, she concentrated and tightened the reins. Then she let Giaccomo gallop toward the first steep jump.

"Now, show them what you can do," she whispered in his ear. A tremble went through the horse's body and, as if he understood, he achieved a speed that made the spectators gasp.

Marina seemed to almost disappear into the waving mane of the huge horse as he jumped over the oxer – a spread fence – without hesitation.

Just over the jump, it seemed as though Giaccomo changed direction in midair, even before his hooves touched the ground. There! The double combination! He flew over the two obstacles with ease, as though they didn't exist.

Ricki held her breath, and dug her fingers into Kevin's arm with each jump that Giaccomo took.

"He's going too fast, Kevin, much too fast! If Marina doesn't slow him down he'll crash right into the triple combination! Why isn't she slowing him down?" she whispered. Ricki had to force herself to keep her eyes open as the horse raced toward the obstacles at a breakneck pace.

Ricki bit her lower lip until it was almost bloody as Giaccomo jumped effortlessly over the first fence of the triple combination. "I can't look!" The teenager swallowed hard, and even Kevin held his breath. At the last moment, Marina gave the horse the signal to spring over the middle fence. They heard the sound of the hooves hitting the top pole , but although the pole wobbled, it stayed put.

"Now it's coming!" groaned Ricki, and pressed her face against Kevin's shoulder. She expected to hear the sound of wood splitting on the third jump, but nothing like that happened.

Meanwhile, Giaccomo raced over the last obstacle of the course, and there was wild applause for the first ride without any faults as Marina rode across the end line on Giaccomo.

"You can look now, Ricki!" said Kevin to his girlfriend,

his voice a little shaky with excitement. Ricki looked up. She had tears in her eyes.

"She made it? She really made it? Marina, you are one heck of a rider!" she called happily to her friend, who was just leaving the arena.

"No faults and the fastest speed! Congratulations! The two of you were awesome! That's going to be hard to beat!" Kevin's eyes shone, as though he himself had ridden the difficult course.

Crissy came running over, too, and congratulated her friend. "I don't think I've ever seen a ride like that, honest!"

Marina jumped down from the saddle. Her knees were trembling. "Phew! I almost lost my nerve at the triple combination," she laughed and hugged the horse.

"You aren't serious, are you?" asked Ricki, but Marina nodded.

"Totally serious! I could almost see myself in the hospital with Maggie in a double bed, but this horse ... I can't find the words."

"He's just wonderful!" Suddenly a man's voice finished the young woman's sentence.

Ricki and Kevin turned around fast and stared at Vera and Larry Bratton, who were standing right behind them.

Larry smiled admiringly at Marina, who returned his look, a little embarrassed. "I hope you're not angry that I changed the registration, but I thought, that Maggie ..."

Larry shook his head. "You don't owe me any explanations. I know that you only rode to show me how wrong I've been about Giaccomo, didn't you?"

Marina blushed, as she slowly nodded.

"You knew, didn't you?" Larry looked at his wife, who just smiled at him. "Otherwise you wouldn't have gone to such lengths to get me to come here with you."

"Of course, you stubborn old mule. You would never have come on your own. Maybe now that you've seen this you can tell your daughter how impressed you are with her horse."

Larry Bratton nodded and stroked Giaccomo gently over his soft, velvety muzzle, which was still trembling.

"I was an idiot," he whispered to the wonderful horse, before he turned to Vera. "Would it be all right with you if we drove to the hospital now to visit Maggie?"

"Of course!" Vera smiled at Marina knowingly, and then she took her husband's arm and the two of them left the show grounds together.

"You knew that Marina was going to ride, didn't you?" Ricki looked fixedly at Kevin.

"Yeah!"

"Rascal!"

Kevin grinned and gave Ricki a kiss on the tip of her nose.

"Hey, did we miss anything?" Cathy and Lillian ran up to them and suddenly stopped short when they saw Marina on Giaccomo. "What's going on?" asked a puzzled Cathy.

Lillian hit her forehead with her hands. "You jumped with Giaccomo and we didn't see you? I can't believe it!"

"And? How did it go?" Cathy asked.

"Well, I'd say you two missed the best ride of the day," replied Ricki and pointed to Marina and Giaccomo. "I'll be very surprised if the two of them haven't already won the advanced jumping event," she announced confidently.

"Ricki, there are still riders to go, and you're already talking about a win," objected Cathy, but Ricki just dismissed her.

"You didn't see how Giaccomo performed. I'm telling you, they've got first place!"

"You know what," interjected Marina finally. "It's not important whether we got first place or not. The main thing is that Maggie's father finally realized what's important. Which means that Giaccomo has won his right to be part of the Bratton family, and that's the biggest prize of the day! That's all I wanted. Ricki, could you please hold Giaccomo's reins for a minute? I think I'm going to be sick."

Ricki just had time to take Giacco's reins as Marina ran off. All the tension had made her stomach rebel.

"I hope it isn't a tie, because Giaccomo would have to do the next ride alone," said Ricki, grinning.

"I'd probably have given up halfway through the first round!" laughed Kevin.

"Kevin, you're going to give the supposed stronger gender a bad name," joked Lillian. But Kevin just smiled.

"Maybe, but at least I'm honest!" he said, and was happy when Ricki gave him a hug.

"I like that much better," she admitted. "And as a reward, you may invite me to have a soda!" teased Ricki.

Kevin groaned. "Once again, honesty doesn't pay, it just makes your wallet smaller."